A New Beginning

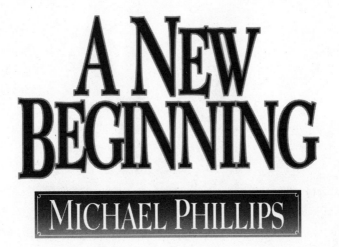

A NEW BEGINNING

MICHAEL PHILLIPS

BETHANY HOUSE PUBLISHERS
MINNEAPOLIS, MINNESOTA 55438

A New Beginning
Copyright © 1997
Michael Phillips

Cover illustration by William Graf

Scripture quotations identified KJV are from the King James Version of the Bible.

Published by Bethany House Publishers
A Ministry of Bethany Fellowship, Inc.
11300 Hampshire Avenue South
Minneapolis, Minnesota 55438

Printed in the United States of America.

Library of Congress Cataloging-in-Publication Data

Phillips, Michael R., 1946–
   A new beginning / Michael Phillips.
      p. m . —(The journals of Corrie & Christopher ; Book 2)
   ISBN 1–55661–945–6   —ISBN 1–55661–933–2 (pbk.)
   I. Title. II. Series: Phillips, Michael R., 1946–   Journals of
Corrie & Christopher ; 2.
PS3566.H492N48   1996
813'54—dc21   96–45914
                                                        CIP

To the Reverend Sam Kleinsasser,
from whose early life Christopher's story,
much of it factual, is drawn—
Pastor who baptized me,
Mentor who nurtured me,
Friend who loved me—
a man whose character and worldwide ministry
constantly remind me that *all* men and women,
whatever their background, can be used mightily by our Father.

CONTENTS

CHAPTER 1

TWO CHANGES

If life didn't contain change, I don't suppose it would be very interesting. Change is the thing that brings about decisions. Decisions call for choices, and without choices to make a person can't grow.

The only trouble is, most of the time it's the *difficult* changes and the *hard* choices you face that make you grow the most. It's not easy to be happy and thankful sometimes when circumstances bring change. You might look back later and realize you grew and matured through them, but at the time all you can think of is how hard it is.

The first change to come into our lives didn't have to do with me. The second one did.

My brother Zack took the job as the new sheriff of Miracle Springs. That was the first one.

We women didn't like the idea too much. But Pa and my other brother Tad and Uncle Nick thought it was great. It was obvious Pa was mighty proud of his son. He and Uncle Nick would joke with each other about coming West to get away from the law—and now they were living under the same roof with the law! Before Zack even had the badge pinned on his vest, Tad was already talking about becoming his deputy. All my stepmother Almeda and my sister Becky and I could think of was the danger a sheriff might have to face . . . and a deputy too.

"There's nothing to worry about," Zack kept saying. "Simon hasn't had to use his gun since the gold rush days."

"Zack's right," Pa added with a laugh. "Why, he told me himself that he has to oil his gun to keep it from rusting up! Sheriffin's an administrative job these days."

I don't think Almeda was convinced.

Zack took over the job right after Christmas, with the beginning of the new year 1868. Simon Rafferty, the old sheriff who had just retired, still came into town from his ranch almost every day just to make sure Zack got off to a good start. He made it clear that Zack could call on him any time if he needed help with something, and that made it a little easier on all of us.

The other big change about to come to the Hollister-Braxton home in Miracle Springs had to do with my new husband, Christopher Braxton, and me. The Braxton half of the clan was planning to pull up stakes and leave the Hollister half to itself again. And this time I wouldn't be on the Hollister side of the fence, but the Braxton side.

Christopher and I waited until two weeks after Christmas—for the season to pass and for Zack to get situated in his new job—before telling the rest of the family what Christopher felt the Lord was showing him—that we were to leave Miracle Springs and return to the East. We would be making plans to leave California early in the spring.

We made the announcement one day at supper. After Christopher finished, everyone sat stone-faced and absolutely silent. I was looking down at my plate. None of my family could believe what they'd heard. The silence went on for several minutes. No one took another bite.

At last I heard someone start to cry softly. I knew it was Becky, and I glanced up.

"But . . . I don't *want* you to leave again, Corrie," she said in a forlorn tone.

"We have to do what the Lord wants," I said, trying to be brave and sound spiritual, but my voice trembled. It was what I thought I *should* say, though the words felt rather hollow. I didn't want to leave Miracle Springs either.

"I missed you so much the last time you were gone," Becky added. "Who will I have to talk to?"

I didn't know what to say. I glanced helplessly at Christopher.

After he had become such a friend to Becky, and after the long talk he and I had had with her a few months earlier about being content not being married, it seemed now we were about to abandon her. I know that's how it appeared to Becky, anyway, and neither Christopher nor I were anxious to say something like, "The Lord will provide you someone," which could only sound rather superficial in her ears. It's all well and good to give someone advice, but then you have to back it up, and I know it must have seemed to Becky that we weren't going to back up ours.

"You can talk to *me!*" suddenly piped up Ruth enthusiastically from her seat beside Becky. It was silent for just an instant. Almeda smiled, and even Becky saw the humor in it and now laughed lightly through her tears.

"Certainly," she said, putting her arm around my eleven-year-old half sister. "How could I have forgotten? Thank you, Ruth—of course I shall talk to you."

Ruth beamed as though she had solved the whole world's problem. Everyone was glad for the diversion in the conversation. A little more laughter followed, and the subject of our leaving did not come up again. But I thought it strange at the time that Almeda didn't say something further. Maybe she could sense how hard the whole situation was for me.

Neither was it something Christopher and I talked much about in the weeks that followed. We just gradually made preparations. He wrote to San Francisco for ticket information and I began thinking of what we should take. We didn't have much—just our clothes and quilts and dishes and a few pieces of furniture we had collected to furnish the little bunkhouse on my family's property where we lived. But we would need at least some of those things to start our new life in the East. So I started saving containers that came into the Hollister Supply Company, our family business, to box and crate up our things.

Jesse Harris—the former outlaw who'd been wounded outside the house the previous fall and had been with us convalescing ever since—had been taking his meals at the table with us for several weeks now. That was another big change that happened, partly in our lives, but mostly in Mr. Harris's life. He'd never been part of a group of people who acted like a *family*. The closest thing he'd ever known was the Catskill Gang. But even though those men rode together, they were still out for themselves.

Mr. Harris couldn't get used to the way we all shared together and prayed about decisions. He had changed a lot since asking the Lord to be part of his life, but it was hard for him to understand what all the fuss was about Christopher and me leaving. He'd always done whatever came into his mind to do.

CHAPTER 2

THE NEW SHERIFF

By the end of the year, Mr. Harris had recuperated from his wounds enough to get up and move around pretty good. It had taken longer than Doc Shoemaker had figured it ought to. He said it was probably because Mr. Harris wasn't very fit in the first place, drinking so much and not eating well. So we did our best to get as much healthy food down him as we could, and of course not a drop of alcohol passed his lips. By Christmas he'd put on probably ten or fifteen pounds and his face showed some color.

No one talked much about it, but we all knew that eventually something was going to have to happen because there were still warrants out for his arrest. Pa had been spending lots of hours alone with Mr. Harris in the bedroom where he lay. None of the rest of us heard any of those conversations, but they were ones Mr. Harris sure never forgot, because he'd often later refer back to one thing or another that Pa'd told him.

A few days after Christmas Sheriff Rafferty came to see Zack. They spoke quietly amongst themselves at one end of the sitting room. When Sheriff Rafferty got up to leave, all I heard him say as they approached the door was, "You sure?"

"Yep, I'll handle it," replied Zack.

As soon as the sheriff was gone, Zack went into the bedroom.

"How you feeling, Mr. Harris?" he asked.

"Near like new, young Hollister. These women o' yers takin' mighty good care o' me."

"That's what I want to talk to you about, Mr. Harris," said

Zack. "You know it's near time you were leaving."

"Yep—I reckoned it was coming sooner or later."

"You know what that means?"

"Don't worry, son," said Mr. Harris. "Your pa an' me, we done talked all about it. Bein' accountable—that's what your pa calls it. I reckon he's right too. I know I gotta own up t' my past and pay fer the wrong I done. If I'm gonna git my life straightened around, ain't no time to waste doing things like I used to. I know well enough where my new home'll be soon's I leave here."

Zack nodded, and they talked a little more.

So it turned out that Zack's first job as sheriff was to transfer Mr. Harris from our house to the jail in town. That's what Sheriff Rafferty had come to talk to him about, offering to do it before the first of the year if Zack wanted. I think he halfway expected trouble. But knowing the man he had shot well enough by this time, Zack said it would not be a problem and that he would handle it alone. I think Zack needed to carry out this first assignment for the sake of his own confidence—and to show the people of Miracle Springs that he was prepared to be their sheriff, whatever came his way.

On the second of January, Zack loaded Mr. Harris into a two-seater buggy, then the two of them set off for town. Zack was now wearing the badge on his vest and his gun on his hip, which I still couldn't get used to. But he didn't take any extra precautions with Mr. Harris, like handcuffs or tying his hands or anything. Even writing that sounds funny, because in the months he had been in our house Mr. Harris had become our friend. Yet still, as he and Zack rode off, with Pa and the rest of us watching them go just a little bit uneasily, there was still no way around the fact that the one man was a sheriff and the other was an outlaw who had come to town in the first place vowing to kill both Zack and Pa.

But Mr. Harris really had changed. Nothing happened, and they made it to town just fine.

But something else *did* happen, and it wasn't that much later either.

No one expected anything so dramatic so soon. Sheriff Rafferty hadn't encountered a dangerous incident in years, and within Zack's first month, he almost . . .

Well—I should tell you about it as it happened.

I was at the supply company—which most of us still called the freight company from its days as the Parrish Mine and Freight—for the day, both working and gathering up some crates and boxes in the wagon to take home for packing. I had just loaded one of them up into the back of the wagon when I saw a stranger ride up and dismount in front of the Gold Nugget saloon down the street. The first thing I noticed was that his horse and saddle weren't cared for. A lot of men don't own much of anything, but at least they keep their horses brushed and their saddles oiled.

I shuddered when I saw him. I could tell he was a bad man. I don't like to say that about anyone God has made. I don't suppose anyone is *really* bad through and through because God says we're made in his image. But from the look on this man's face I didn't see too much left of whatever goodness of God's image might have once been in him.

He walked into the saloon and I went back into the freight company.

I'd just about forgotten about the incident. Ten minutes or so passed. Suddenly I heard yelling outside.

"Hey, you in there!" called a loud voice from the street. "Yeah, inside the jail. . . ."

The instant I heard the word *jail*, my heart leapt into my throat. I dropped what I was doing and ran to the window. There was the man I had seen, now standing in the middle of the street facing the sheriff's office!

"I'm talking to you, Sheriff! I'm calling you out," yelled the man in an angry tone. "You got my partner in there in your jail, and I want him."

A second or two of silence followed. My eyes were as big as saucers. I was terrified but didn't know what I could do. I didn't even think to pray. I just stood there at the window hoping Zack wouldn't come out.

But slowly the door of his office opened. Zack walked slowly out onto the board sidewalk, then stopped, just looking at the man.

There was still that holster and gun at his side, and I liked it less now than ever!

"Jesse Harris is your partner?" asked Zack calmly.

"Ain't the name I knowed him by—but you got him in there all right. I heard. An' you either bring him out t' me, or else I'll have t' go in there an' git him myself."

"I'm afraid I can't do that, mister," said Zack.

The man laughed.

"Where's the sheriff, deputy? My business is with him."

"I'm the sheriff."

The man laughed again, this time with cruel derision in his tone.

"Come on now, son, before you git yerself hurt—just let my partner go and you can run along home."

"I told you before, I can't do that."

"Yer just a blamed kid!" the man said, still laughing. This was going to be easier than he'd thought! "Who's gonna stop me?"

"If I have to, I will."

Suddenly the man's laughter stopped and his face took on a deadly expression.

"Now look, kid, I ain't got all day." As he spoke his fingers began to inch imperceptibly toward his gun. I saw his fingers twitching ever so slightly.

Before I knew what I was doing, I opened the door and ran out.

"Zack!" I screamed.

"Get back, Corrie!" shouted Zack. His voice was different than I'd ever heard it. Even as Zack spoke to me, I saw that he never took his eyes off the stranger. His face was calm but his eyes had a squint to them, and I knew he was watching the man's hand.

I stopped in my tracks, terrified for what might happen. Out of the corner of my eyes I saw a few people creeping out of the stores and saloons up and down the street. We'd heard about things like this, but there'd never been so dramatic a showdown right in the middle of Miracle Springs.

"Come on now, kid," said the stranger, "I don't wanna have t' kill you. But I don't aim t' leave this two-bit town till I got my partner, one way or another. Now bring him out, I tell you, before I have t' get rough with you."

Zack didn't say a word. Not a muscle on his body moved.

Suddenly the man went for his gun.

I screamed and ran toward them.

It was all over in a second or two. Only one shot rang out, dust flew, several yells and shouts sounded, and within seconds the street filled with thirty or forty people running forward into the street.

Nobody had even seen Zack's hand move—that's how fast he'd drawn his gun. The gunfire I'd heard was his. The stranger lay writhing in pain in the middle of the street, shouting out obscenities. A crowd gathered around him as Zack now approached. The people stood back to let him through, looking at him with a sudden new awe and respect, as if they'd never seen him before.

Nobody had any idea Zack was so fast with a gun!

I wanted to run up and throw my arms around him for sheer joy. I'd been afraid he was going to get shot. But I stopped myself, all at once seeing him differently, like the rest of the folks I suppose. I realized he wasn't just my little brother anymore. He was the *sheriff*, and I couldn't just go up and hug the sheriff after a gunfight!

"Who is it?" mumbled some of the onlookers.

"Don't know . . . never seen him before."

"Where'd he come from?"

Zack reached the center of the crowd about the same time Doc Shoemaker did. The man on the ground was holding his right shoulder with his other hand. He realized he was bleeding pretty bad, so he gradually quit swearing and let the doctor take a look at him. Doc stooped down and looked the man over.

"Better get him over to my place," he said to a few of the men. "Don't want him to bleed to death out here in the street."

"Send somebody over for me when you got him patched up, Doc," said Zack. "I'll come over and fetch him."

"What you gonna do with him, Zack?" somebody asked.

"Put him in the jail," answered Zack. "As far as I know, trying to kill a sheriff's against the law."

He turned and walked back to his office. Doc Shoemaker and a couple of the men lifted the stranger to his feet while the crowd slowly disbursed. Nobody talked about anything else the rest of the day, and by evening news of the incident had spread for miles.

I guess Miracle Springs really did have a new sheriff!

CHAPTER 3

ZACK'S TRIUMPH

I don't know how news travels so fast.

Sometimes I think it gets carried by the wind itself, because people seem to find out things faster than a galloping horse can take someone from one place to another to deliver it.

I was so jittery right after the shooting I could hardly finish loading the wagon. It wasn't thirty minutes later before Pa came riding into town with a cloud of dust behind him like he was trying out to be a Pony Express rider like Zack had been.

How in the world he got news of the shooting so fast, like I said, I can't imagine. When Pa arrived I was just about ready to leave for home to tell everyone what had happened.

Pa rode straight to the jail, jumped off his horse, and ran inside. He'd been in there with Zack five or ten minutes when Mr. Saunders came from Doc Shoemaker's to tell Zack the man who had tried to break Mr. Harris out of jail was bandaged up and ready. Pa and Zack came out of the sheriff's office together, with Mr. Saunders following along behind. I just couldn't get over how tall and confident Zack seemed all of a sudden. He looked five years older! He and Pa walked down the street to the doc's just like two grown men.

What am I saying? That's exactly what they were! I reckon what looked so strange was that *Zack* seemed to be leading the way.

A few minutes later they returned, this time with Mr. Harris's partner between them, kind of stumbling along though there was nothing wrong with his legs. His shoulder was bound up in white bandages. I half expected Zack to be holding a gun on him, but I guess it was hardly necessary. He wasn't going to get away from Zack, especially wounded like he was.

Pa went back into the jail building with them. I waited a little while, but Pa didn't come out again, so I figured I might as well go on home.

Pa got back a couple hours after I did. We were still all in the house talking about it. Then as soon as Pa walked in, the hubbub started all over again.

Zack came home for supper about six.

Everybody'd been waiting for him, but he walked in and sat down like nothing had happened. The whole house was silent. Ruth stared at him as if she suddenly didn't know it was Zack but was looking at somebody more famous than she'd ever seen.

Zack glanced around. Every eye of the whole family was glued on him.

"What?" he laughed.

"Well?" said Almeda expectantly.

"Well what? What in tarnation're you all staring at?"

"Tell us about it, Zack, for heaven's sake!"

"Nothing much to tell," he replied nonchalantly. "I figured Pa and Corrie'd have told you what happened by now. Corrie saw the whole thing."

"I did," I said, "and all I want to know is how you got so fast drawing a gun?"

"I don't know—practice, I reckon."

"How fast was it, Corrie?" asked Tad. He'd already heard me describe the scene at least three times.

"Like lightning," I said. "It was so fast I tell you I didn't see Zack's hand actually move. It happened too fast to see."

"And the other man drew first?"

"He did," I replied. "But his gun had hardly cleared his holster before it went flying out of his hand from Zack's shot."

"Whole town's talking about it, that's for sure," said Pa, now adding his own slightly less than eyewitness account.

"Show us, Zack," said Ruth. "Show us how you did it."

"Shush, dear," said Almeda. "Your big brother's an important man now. Sheriffs don't go around showing off their draw. It's just part of their work—a tool, same as a pickax is for a miner. Now, gather round, everyone. Supper's getting cold."

"Well, I reckon you put me in my place," laughed Pa, getting up from his chair.

"How so?" asked Zack.

"I don't even want to tell you after today," said Pa. "But the truth is, when Simon came to talk to me about you being sheriff, I admit I didn't like the idea much at first. I wasn't sure you were ready. I hate to say it, but it looks like he knew my own son better'n I did! He knew you could handle the job and he told me so."

Zack grinned.

"Tarnation!" Pa exclaimed. "I'm the father of the tough new sheriff of Miracle Springs!"

"I *was* a little nervous," Zack finally admitted.

"You sure didn't show it," I said.

"It's because of you, Pa," said Zack, "that I was able to be so calm."

"How's that?"

"From watching you standing right out there on our porch talking to Mr. Harris—you know, when he came looking for us."

"Who's watching the two men now, son?" Pa asked as we sat down.

"Smitty," replied Zack. "I gotta go back into town. I have to spend the night there till the marshal's through and decides what to do with Unger."

"That's his name, Unger?"

Zack nodded. "Mr. Harris calls him Curly."

"Hmm . . . Curly Unger—doesn't mean a thing to me."

"From what I can tell listening to them talk," said Zack, "I don't think they've been riding together too long."

"Well, I knew our lives were changing," said Almeda as she dished out helpings of stew onto everyone's plates. "Change can be good, but sometimes it brings things we never expect, and I certainly didn't expect something like *this*! Zack, you be careful, you hear me."

"Yes, ma'am," laughed Zack. "I always try to be."

Christopher had been noticeably silent the whole time. Especially after Almeda's comment about change, I could tell he was thinking about something. As soon as supper was over, he excused himself and left the house. I got up a minute or two after and went outside.

I saw Christopher walking alone, heading up the stream into the woods. At first I started to follow him, then some inner sense told me he was probably praying and that I needed to let him go by himself.

I did not know it at the time, but would find out later, that he was still struggling with the decision he had made. I was struggling with it too, of course, but in my own way, and I had no idea what Christopher was thinking and praying about. As much as we thought we communicated—and we did too—we were learning that there are times when it is very difficult to open up what is in your heart, even to the person you love most in all the world.

CHAPTER 4

CHRISTOPHER'S QUANDARY

During the second week of February, little Mary Rutledge came over with the message that her father wanted to see Christopher. Christopher and I rode over to the pastor's house that same afternoon.

"Thank you for coming, Christopher," said Rev. Rutledge after Harriet showed us into the sitting room.

"Is anything wrong?" asked Christopher.

"Oh no—it's nothing, really," he replied. "It's just that I'm still not feeling altogether back to my old self, and I have a favor to ask of you."

"Anything."

"A funeral's come up down at Dutch Flat. I wondered if you'd take care of it for me?"

"Of course, Avery," Christopher replied, "but surely they wouldn't want someone they don't know."

"I'm not acquainted with the family either—new to the area. The request came to the church yesterday. Little girl died—only eight years old—and they want a minister to say some words at the grave site. They'll be just as happy with you as me."

"Well . . . certainly, if you think it would be appropriate."

"It will be, I assure you."

"Then I would be happy to."

"Good, I appreciate it," sighed Rev. Rutledge tiredly. "I just was not up to that ride."

He handed Christopher a sheet of paper.

"Here is everything I was told about the girl. It's not much."

"It will be fine," said Christopher, glancing over the information. "I'll talk to the parents beforehand."

Two mornings later, Christopher set out early for Dutch Flat. Zack went with him, both to show him the way and because he had someone down near there he needed to see on some sheriff matter. On the way the two had a long conversation, which Christopher told me about a couple of months later.

"So you finally got the Unger fellow out of your hair?" said Christopher.

"Yep—he's on his way to Sacramento," replied Zack. "But I tell you, he got an earful before he went."

"How do you mean?" asked Christopher.

"Jesse told him all about the Lord and doing what the Bible says and about praying. They talked for hours, till there were times when Unger had to tell Jesse to just shut up."

Christopher laughed. "A church service right there in the jail."

"That's what it was. Jesse kept trying to get Unger to pray like he had, but Unger would have none of it. He thought Jesse'd gone loco."

"Know any more yet about what will happen to Jesse?"

Zack shook his head. "The marshal's looking into the old warrants. He may have to follow his pal Unger down to the capital. Doesn't seem likely we're gonna just be able to let him go."

"They wouldn't—you don't think . . ."

Christopher couldn't say it, but Zack knew what he was thinking.

"You mean hang him? I don't know—not unless there's a warrant for murder on him. Nothing much we can do but wait and see."

They rode on without saying anything further for a mile or so.

"Mind if I ask you a question, Zack?" said Christopher after they had ridden along awhile in silence.

"'Course not—fire away."

"That's a good way of saying it, coming from you," laughed Christopher. "But I suppose it's fitting too, because I wanted to ask you about your becoming sheriff."

Christopher paused a moment.

"How did you know," he went on, "whether you were supposed to take the job or not?"

"How do you mean?" replied Zack. "I thought about it a lot, if that's what you're getting at."

"But how did you know if you were *supposed* to say yes? How did you . . . *know*?"

"You mean, if God wanted me to?"

"Exactly—whether it was the right thing to do."

"I don't know as a body's ever sure completely about that. But shoot, Christopher—what're you asking me for?" laughed Zack. "*You're* the preacher."

"Ex-preacher," corrected Christopher.

"I thought that's why you was going back to the East, because you thought God was telling you your preaching days weren't over after all."

"Yeah," sighed Christopher, "I guess you're right at that."

"So why *are* you asking me?" said Zack again. "I thought preachers knew all about that kind of thing."

"Preachers haven't got any more an open road to God's ear than anyone else. Takes just as much practice for us to hear God's voice—just like you said about learning to draw your gun fast. All good things take practice to learn how to do."

"I don't suppose I ever thought about praying taking practice," said Zack.

"It sure does, especially the most important part of praying—the listening half. That's the hardest part, the aspect of prayer most people aren't too skilled at. It requires a *lot* of practice, and I'm still just learning myself."

Christopher paused. "To answer your question, Zack," he went on after a moment, "the reason I'm asking is because I'm really struggling with my own decision."

"You mean about leaving Miracle Springs?"

Christopher nodded.

"I thought it was all decided."

"I did too, but I find myself still asking the Lord if it really *is* his will or not. Then I think to myself that maybe I just want to please Corrie and that is why I am trying to talk myself out of it. You know she really doesn't want to go?"

26

Zack nodded.

"And by then I am more confused than when I started!" Christopher added, laughing. "I tell you, Zack—this is the toughest decision I've ever faced."

"Why, do you think?" asked Zack.

"I don't know. Sometimes the signals from God just aren't so clear as at other times. He uses circumstances so often to lead us, and I haven't really had much along that line to go on."

"I suppose that's one of the reasons I felt that the sheriff's job was right," said Zack, "now that you mention it. I'd actually found myself thinking about the possibility someday—on account of the fact that Mr. Rafferty was getting on in years. When he and the mayor came to talk to me and offered me the job, I reckon I took that as a sign that I might be supposed to do it."

"I agree that circumstances like that ought to be listened to. It doesn't mean something *is* God's will, only that it *might* be. Circumstances don't always indicate the direction God wants us to take, but they do always indicate that God is at work. They remind us to perk up our ears and listen intently."

"A good way of putting it," smiled Zack.

"But as much as I perk up my ears in this particular case, I just don't seem to be hearing much!" laughed Christopher. "Only the sense that a change is coming and that somehow ministry is to be more a part of my life again."

"Like doing this funeral you're headed to?"

"I suppose so, except that I have the feeling it will be more involved than that—although perhaps this is one of those circumstances that has something to say to me . . . if only I knew what it was!"

They rode along for some time in silence. As they did, Christopher's thoughts turned toward prayer and he found himself quietly talking to the Lord in his heart.

Lord, I need to hear your voice, he prayed. *I feel you calling me back into the ministry. I know you have a place where you want me involved in men's and women's lives. I know you are trustworthy and that I can count on you to do your work. But I also know that perhaps I need to step out and do something—but what? Honor Corrie, Lord, for her support during this difficult decision and this difficult move. Please provide some further sign that I am doing the right thing, or else bring circumstances to bear upon me that will stay my hand and speak otherwise to me. I am trying to listen, Lord . . . help me to hear.*

CHAPTER 5

FUNERAL AT DUTCH FLAT

". . . would like in closing to offer this brief quotation," said Christopher, then paused, took up a small volume from the stand in front of him, and flipped through its pages to find the passage.

Ten feet in front of him sat a plain wooden casket at the edge of the grave where it would soon be laid to rest. Gathered around and behind it were ten or twelve of the residents of the Dutch Flat area. Beside the casket, dressed in black, stood the father and mother and older brother of the departed girl, mother weeping occasionally, father standing stoically as he considered his duty.

"I realize," said Christopher after a moment, "that the one thing a minister attempts to do in a situation such as this—bring comfort—is the one thing which is in a sense an impossibility under the circumstances. Yet I believe there is comfort to be gained if we can only lift our eyes a moment, raise them from the grave here in the ground, a hole which seems cold and uninviting, and raise our sight instead up to the horizon. Perhaps there are rays of sunlight streaming down from behind the clouds. Can we not try, my friends, even in our grief, to envision these rays not as coming down but as going *up*, as a grand stairway up from this grave to the heavens?

"Cast your gaze up and imagine if you can a faint image of your daughter ascending that stairway to her new home. I say *imagine* it, for our mortal eyes cannot see it. Yet I tell you such *is* indeed the reality of this moment. This grave is not the future home of young Jessica Porter. Neither does this casket before us anymore hold her. It holds her earthly clothes . . . but not *her*. Gaze up, not down, for even now she ascends that heavenly stairway. And look, there are the angels coming down to meet her, taking her hand that they might lead her up to her new home."

Christopher paused. The girl's mother wept, more noticeably now.

"What I would like to read, then," he went on, "are words written for just such an occasion as this. They were penned by one seeking to comfort a friend who, like you here today, had lost a child—in this particular case, a son. The author reminds his friend that God loves our loved ones even more than we, and reminds him further that death must not break the bonds of love, but rather should strengthen them. Let me read."

Christopher glanced down at the book, then began. " 'Dear friend,' " he read,

> *What can I say to you, for the hand of the Lord is heavy upon you. But it is his hand, and the very heaviness of it is good. There is but one thought that can comfort, and that is that God is immeasurably more the father of our children than we are. It is all because he is our Father that we are fathers. It is well to say, "The Lord gave and the Lord hath taken away," but it is not enough. We must add, "And the Lord will give again." He takes that he may give more closely—make more ours. Let me say, then, that I believe the bond is henceforth closer between you and your son.*

He paused again, closed the book, then picked up another slender volume he had brought.

"Let me close," he said, "by reading a few lines from a Scottish poet." Again he found his place and began:

> *To give a thing and take again*
> *Is counted meanness among men;*
> *Still less to take what once is given*
> *Can be the royal way of heaven.*
> *But human hearts are crumbly stuff,*
> *And never, never love enough;*
> *And so God takes and, with a smile,*
> *Puts our best things away awhile.*

> *Some therefore weep, some rave, some scorn;*
> *Some wish they never had been born;*
> *Some humble grow at last and still,*
> *And then God gives them what they will.*

"Let us pray. *Our dear, loving heavenly Father, increase our trust in your love. May we learn even to trust you in death. May we trust that you are more the Father of our loved ones than we are. Give us spiritual eyes, our Father, to see that this grave is not the resting place of this dear child, but that you are already gathering Jessica smiling into your arms and welcoming her to her new home, the home of your presence, the home of your heart. We thank you, Father, that you are good . . . and that we may trust you for all things, even in death. Amen.*"

Tears now flowed freely down the faces of both father and mother. They came forward while their friends moved slowly about in the background and spoke in hushed tones.

"We cannot thank you enough," said Mrs. Porter, taking Christopher's hand. "Everything you said was very meaningful."

"You have helped us a great deal, Mr. Braxton," said Mr. Porter. "It has been a struggle to come to terms with why this happened. Listening to you just now, I realized that we must look beyond *why*, that *trust* must be greater than our powers of reasoning."

Christopher smiled, and the two men shook hands.

"You do not, if you will pardon my saying so, strike me as a typical Westerner," said Christopher. "You sound like someone I might have encountered at a philosophical society meeting in the East."

Mr. Porter smiled. "We are new here," he said, "and, yes, I suppose you might say we are of a more intellectual bent than most men and women we have met thus far. I mean no disrespect in saying such a thing, only that I am aware that there is a difference."

"I understand," said Christopher.

"I think that is what was so helpful in what you said here today," now put in Mrs. Porter. "We have not heard such a sermon, if you will, since our arrival. If *you* will pardon *my* saying so, you sound more like an eastern preacher yourself."

"Tell me," asked Mr. Porter, "when are your services up in

Miracle Springs? We would very much like to attend and listen to more of what you have to say."

"Actually," replied Christopher, "I am not myself the pastor. Rev. Rutledge was ill and asked me to come here today. You are right," he added, turning to Mrs. Porter, "I am an eastern preacher—from Virginia. My wife and I are leaving next month to return there."

"Oh, I see . . . hmm, that is too bad. Well, nevertheless, we are very grateful that you were able to attend to our daughter's burial today."

CHAPTER 6

TRUSTWORTHINESS

By late February the plans for Christopher and me to leave Miracle Springs were well in motion.

I wished the transcontinental railroad were finished and we could be among the first people to ride it. But Christopher purchased tickets for the third week of March on a ship bound from San Francisco to New York City. We didn't exactly know where we would go from there, but we tentatively planned to settle somewhere in Virginia.

I did my best to keep a cheerful outlook, though the thought of leaving Miracle Springs could still bring tears to my eyes if I let it. I tried not to think about it. I wish I could have anticipated the move as a great adventure. I know that is what it would have been for most people. But this wasn't going to be like before, when I had traveled east to help with the war effort. The fact that this would be a permanent move, not just a temporary visit, changed everything. What if I never saw my family again? I couldn't bear even to think of such a thing.

So I cannot say this was an easy time for me. Thinking about this move was probably the hardest thing I had ever had to face as a Christian. I had more or less come to terms with the decision before Christmas, but I still had to pray every day for the ability to trust both God and Christopher.

When Christopher told me about the funeral in Dutch Flat and about what he'd tried to communicate about God being trustworthy, I found myself thinking about my life and my own reaction to our upcoming move. I realized the reason I'd finally been able to lay down my own wishes in the matter was because I did trust Christopher. I knew him to be trustworthy. This did not necessarily mean that I believed he would always be right. God, of course, we trust because we know he *will* always do the right thing. He is perfect, we are not. But we can still find human beings *trustworthy*, even though at the same time we know that anyone can make a mistake.

So maybe Christopher would make mistakes. Maybe he might even be mistaken about our moving to the East. If I knew him to be trustworthy, then that almost didn't matter anymore. His trustworthiness was higher than whether he was right or wrong in a given situation.

At least that is how I came to see it. This realization helped me to say to the Lord one last time, and this time with more contentment, *Not my will, but yours be done.*

I tried to explain to Christopher the thoughts I'd had.

"I know you have been struggling with the decision," he said. "But you have shown me, at the same time, that you have trusted me in spite of your doubts."

"I could never question your trustworthiness," I said, "and eventually I came to see that to be a higher thing than the decision itself."

"You cannot know how much that means," replied Christopher quietly and sincerely, "and how much I appreciate it. I don't know if a woman is capable of knowing how much trust means to a man. I realize that there are cads and untrustworthy men in plenty, and I don't suppose *they* ought to be trusted. But for a woman to find a man honest and trustworthy to an extent that she is able to rely on him and place her confidence in him, as you have done with me—that means more than you can know."

"Thank you," I said. "I suppose I didn't know how much it meant."

"And you know, Corrie," Christopher went on, "that may even be one of the reasons I've been in such a quandary over my decision."

"Because I trusted you?"

Christopher nodded. "In a way, your trust makes it all the

harder. Because if you *hadn't* trusted me so much, or perhaps if you had expressed your dissatisfaction more persistently and kept saying you thought I was wrong . . . well, that might have pushed me even further in the other direction, forcing me to defend the decision I had made within myself. Do you see what I mean?"

"Not exactly."

"I think as soon as others say or imply that he might be wrong, a person subconsciously builds up a fortress of reasoning to defend a position he's taken. I don't say it's good to do that—it's not. It clouds your judgment and your openness. I only say that such is a normal human tendency. But your trusting me rather than arguing against my decision, trusting and sacrificing your own—"

"Aren't you spiritualizing my position just a bit?" I interrupted. "I promised to stay with you till death do us part. I've done nothing more than any wife would do."

"No, Corrie. You are staying with me in soul and spirit. Many wives stay with their husbands in body but leave soul and spirit behind. We've both seen plenty of wives who are here in California with their husbands, yet never really let go of the East. And they never let their husbands forget that they don't like it here. They never allow themselves the freedom of trusting their husband's decision. You know the proverb about a quarrelsome or nagging wife?"

I nodded. "But how does trust make it *harder* for you?"

"Because since I haven't been forced into defending what I feel the Lord is telling me, I am all the more concerned that I truly *am* listening to him. I'm having to muster up all the old sermons I preached about knowing God's will and try now to apply them in my own life!"

"Zack used to tell about the time he was being chased by the Paiutes and trying to recall a sermon Rev. Rutledge had preached on knowing what to do. I still laugh when I think about it."

"I think I've heard the story too—something about closing his eyes and counting and hoping the Indians would disappear."

"It is so funny to hear him tell it!"

"Let's close our eyes and see where *we* wind up."

We did so.

"Well, where do you have us?" asked Christopher after a minute, "in Virginia or California?"

"Wherever *you* are," I said.

"That's not fair," laughed Christopher, tickling me in the ribs.

We began laughing. At length we lay down on the bed, and Christopher put out his right arm and I laid my head on his shoulder. He wrapped his arm around me. We were quiet for a few moments, then he began to pray.

"Lord," he said, *"whatever else is to come to us, I want to thank you for what a precious gift Corrie is, and thank you again for giving her to me. We continue to ask you to guide our thoughts and our decisions in this important time of change in our lives."*

Even as he was praying I found myself smiling as I remembered again how Christopher had found his "gift"—lying unconscious on a Virginia roadside, and with a bullet hole in her! God had brought us so far and so faithfully from those dangerous wartime days.

How could I not trust him to be faithful with us now?

CHAPTER 7

MEMORIES

Becky and I were sitting at the table after breakfast one morning. All the others had left on their day's business. Ruth sat on the rug near the fire while Almeda sat on a chair behind her and began gathering her long hair into two braids. About halfway down Ruth's back she joined the two braids into one thick one for the rest of the way.

I was in no hurry to go back out to the bunkhouse to continue my packing. It was a cold morning and I decided to have an extra cup of tea instead. There'd been a light frost during the night, and it felt good to be warm inside and out. Pa'd set a great blaze going in the fireplace before he left, and the kitchen was already feeling toasty. Becky just sat at the table, absently making patterns on her plate with biscuit crumbs and drying bits of egg yolk.

"I'm going to miss all this," I said at length, not talking to anyone in particular. "I don't mind telling you that I'm a little nervous about leaving. How long does it take for someone to make a nice cozy home like this?"

"It doesn't take any time at all," replied Almeda. "By the time you make your first hot meal and fill your new home with appetizing smells and spread out your quilts by the fire, you'll have a cozy home."

"What if I can't do it?"

"Anyone can make a place cozy, Corrie. Because it's not the place, it's being with your man and knowing you love each other."

"I remember when Pa and Uncle Nick first brought us here

when there was just a cabin. I made biscuits then, but it didn't feel cozy. We were nervous and scared."

"That's because you hadn't yet learned to love your pa like you do now. Love is what makes a home."

"I don't remember it being so bad, Corrie," said Becky. "You made it feel like a home for me. I remember thinking it was great to be with Pa and Uncle Nick again and having someplace besides the wagon to sleep in. And besides, you always made such good biscuits."

I couldn't help smiling at Becky's younger and more innocent memories of a time that had been very difficult for me as the oldest of five children whose mother had just died.

"You see, Corrie," said Almeda, "Becky knew that you loved her and that you would watch after her. You made it a home for Becky and the others. You might have been scared, but you were taking care of the young ones, and they felt safe."

I was quiet a moment, holding my cup of warm tea between my hands, thinking back to those early days in Miracle Springs. They seemed a lifetime away. Then my memories drifted even further back to our days of living in New York, days I knew Tad could hardly remember. I had been fifteen when that part of my life had changed and we'd come West. Now Miracle Springs had been my home for fifteen years, and I was about to embark on another great change. What would the *next* fifteen years bring, I wondered. Fifteen years from now I would be forty-five. I could hardly imagine it!

It was Becky's voice that brought me out of my reverie.

"Corrie," she said, starting to laugh, "do you remember when Almeda made Pa take us in?"

"I'll never forget. She was determined that he and Uncle Nick were going to take care of us."

"How could Ma make Pa take care of you?" Ruth piped up.

Becky and I looked at each other and now burst out laughing.

"Your mother had a way of making *everybody* do what they ought to, Ruth," I replied.

"Come now, girls, you're making me sound like a bossy old lady!" objected Almeda with a smile just as she finished tying off Ruth's braid with a ribbon.

"You should have seen your ma, Ruth," said Becky, "sitting up there on her freight wagon with her leather breeches and a whip in her hand—why, she could make anybody do anything."

"Girls, you'll put all kinds of wild and silly notions about me into poor Ruth's head!" Even as she said it, however, Almeda joined us in laughter.

"I want to hear more!" said Ruth, thoroughly enjoying the enlightening exchange.

"We need to get you off to school, young lady," said Almeda, standing up.

"Please, Ma, I want to hear more of Corrie's and Becky's stories."

"And what would Miss Benson say if you are not there?"

Ruth sighed and now stood up and reluctantly began helping Almeda gather lunch bucket, jackets, and mittens. In another ten minutes they were gone. Becky and I cleared the table and washed up the dishes. By the time we were through, the morning sun had just about cleared away most of the frost that wasn't lying in the shade, and it looked as though it would be a bright, crisp, clear, sunny day—just the sort of perfect winter's day that happens only in northern California.

"Becky," I suggested, "let's take the horses and go for a ride up into the hills."

"That's the kind of thing that you do!" Becky laughed. "I'm not a horsewoman like you."

"Please. I'll saddle the horses while you write a note to tell the others where we've gone."

"What will I say?"

"That we're riding up to the falls by Forest Glen. I want to show you one of my favorite places. If I'm going to have to leave California, I want *someone* to be able to enjoy it after I'm gone."

CHAPTER 8

SISTERS

It didn't feel like a wintry February day by the time we found ourselves galloping along the road through the trees and foothills that led in the direction I wanted to go. Before we had been gone ten minutes, we had to stop to take off our gloves and unbutton our coats.

"Phew, I forgot how hot you get when you ride hard!" said Becky. "I ride so seldom, I was worried that maybe I'd have forgotten how."

"You never forget how to ride," I answered. "And besides, the horses know what to do."

As the road gradually steepened and narrowed, we slowed to a walk, making our way eastward through the foothills along the side of the swollen creek that flowed down out of the mountains, past our family's mine and our claim (where Pa still hoped to strike gold again) and on into Miracle Springs and down farther into the valley where it eventually fell into the Yuba and Feather Rivers and finally the great Sacramento River itself. It was about a three-mile ride to a place where two smaller creeks joined to create Miracle Springs Creek.

When we got to the fork, we dismounted so the horses could rest a bit and take a drink out of the nice cold mountain stream. Whatever the blue sky and the bright sun might be trying to say, it was definitely winter. The seasons aren't so defined here as in the East, and the pines and firs were nice and green. Yet there was still a different look to the terrain and to the forest and the grasses underfoot. We stood gazing about, drinking in the quiet. No words passed between us. This moment was in such contrast to the chatty time we had spent with Almeda and Ruth earlier. But when you are out in the midst of nature's wonders, a different kind of sharing takes place that requires no words.

In a few minutes we remounted our horses, and I now led the way along one of the two creeks in a more northward direction. After another forty or fifty minutes, we drew near the place I had wanted to show Becky.

I reined in beside a small still pool of dark blue-green water and dismounted. Becky did likewise.

"Do you hear the falls up ahead?" I said.

We were silent. Then Becky nodded. "Yes . . . yes, I think I do. Is it much farther?"

"We're almost there."

I knelt down to take a drink from the pool. "Come, have a drink, Becky," I said. "You've never tasted anything so good!"

Becky knelt down and scooped her hand into the water.

"It's so cold!"

"It's snow-water," I replied. "That's one of the reasons it tastes so good."

We stood and now walked our horses, for the way grew rockier and steeper the closer we got to the falls. Eventually it became even too difficult for them to walk.

"Let's tie the horses here," I said. "There's no room for them at the falls anyway. I usually walk from here up."

We secured the horses, then took our packs of bread and climbed the rest of the way over rocks and up the face of the mountain through the brush until the falls became visible to us. The moment they came into view, both Becky and I were silenced in awe of the long fall of water from the stream over the tall cliff. It plunged straight down, cascaded off a boulder or two in a great white spray, and finally splashed into the deep pool below, which wasn't yet visible from where we stood but beside which, as I had told Becky, was one of my favorite "sitting spots."

"It's so beautiful," said Becky quietly at length. "Now I see why you wanted to bring me here."

"God has made so many places like this," I said, "that are in places where nobody sees them. If I made something this beautiful, I would want to show it to the whole world. But God seems to make things just because they are beautiful. That's enough."

Becky still stood gazing about speechless. "But that makes it all the more wonderful when you chance to find one," she said finally. "You must feel as though this is your own private beautiful place, that God made just for you."

"I have felt that," I said. "And now it is *our* special beautiful place. Promise me you'll ride up here in the summer to see it. There's not so much water then, but lush moss and wild flowers grow everywhere. Promise me you'll come."

"Oh, I will!"

"I'll be in the East thinking about you sitting here under the cool spray on a hot day in July!"

"I will come here often," whispered Becky, her mood growing quiet again. "I understand now why you were always riding off."

We stood a moment more side by side, then gave one another a tight hug.

"I'm going to miss you, Becky," I said.

"And I'm going to miss you. I love you, Corrie. You're the best sister ever."

"And I love you too, Becky. Next to Christopher, you're the best friend I have. But let's walk up closer."

"Is it safe?"

"In the summer and autumn, when there's not so much water, you can even get up behind the falls. Come on, I want to show you the pool!"

I led the way, climbing around a huge boulder to the point where I hoped to show Becky the clearest, bluest pool of mountain water. The falls splashed into one end, but the other had always seemed to me like a blue round saucer holding water for all the forest creatures to come and drink.

As I made my way around the boulder and into sight of the pool, suddenly I froze with a look of horror on my face.

There in the middle of the tranquil blue saucer floated the dead body of a gray mountain deer.

"Oh, eech!" exclaimed Becky. "Corrie, we drank water from that stream!"

My tongue began to salivate even as she said it, and a shiver went down my back.

We stood staring a moment or two longer, then I realized that it wasn't only Becky and me that drank the water that came down from this pool. This stream flowed into the Miracle Springs Creek, past our house, and into town. *Everybody* drank this water.

"Becky," I said, "we've got to get it out of there somehow!"

"What do you mean—how?"

"We can't just leave it there. If this deer remains here, it will eventually bloat and rot and contaminate the spring."

"But what can we possibly do?"

Already I had turned and was looking about for some large sticks or branches. I found a fallen limb from a nearby pine that I thought was long enough. With Becky's help I dragged it down the slope and into the water. It was just long enough to reach the deer. I gave the body several shoves, the last of which sent the branch from my hands floating out across the pond.

"That may do it," I said. "Let's see if we can get around to the other side."

By the time we had scrambled around the water's edge, the deer had floated leisurely from the center of the pond to within six or seven feet of where we now stood.

"One of us is going to have to get into that water and pull it the rest of the way," I said. I sat down and began to take off my boots.

"But, Corrie, the water's too cold!"

"I'll be all right," I said. "Nobody will see us here. When we're done I'll put my dry things back on."

I undressed up to my bloomers, then stepped gingerly into the pool. Quickly I yanked back my foot. Becky was right—the water was cold!

But I had no choice. After a few seconds of gathering up my courage, I plunged my feet in, stepped carefully forward to a depth of about my knees, and then soon was shivering as the water came up to my waist. I was only about five feet from the edge, for the bottom was steep. I reached out as far as I could while retaining my balance, and just barely managed to touch the deer's carcass with my fingers. It made my skin crawl momentarily, but I did my best to pull it toward me. As the dead body began again to float toward me, I backed up the slope and out of the water the way I had come.

A few minutes later I stood on shore again, dripping and shivering, and the deer was floating at the water's edge.

"We've got to try to pull it up and out of the water," I said. "I want you to grab on to one of his hind legs there."

With a determined grimace, Becky did so while I took hold of the two stiff front legs. Pulling and heaving and maneuvering as best we could, in two or three minutes we had managed to haul the thing out of the water and onto the rocky edge of the pool.

Becky grunted again in disgust, then washed off her hands in the water and took several steps away. I washed my hands too, then put my clothes back on. I was freezing and already beginning to think of the nice fire we had left back home! Becky gave me her coat, but it was with great difficulty that I managed to get my boots on, for my fingers were practically frozen.

We wasted no time getting back to our waiting horses, nor in riding down the mountain. I rode as fast as I dared go with Becky, and when we got back, never had I enjoyed a fire and a cup of tea so much.

It took me nearly two hours, with my feet propped up in front of the flame, to finally finish warming up!

I found myself thinking about the incident for a long time after that. Compared with many of the things I had done in my life, I don't suppose this one contained all that much significance, yet I often thought of it in after years. I think it was partly because it happened to Becky and me together, alone and a good ways from home. We'd played together as children, of course, but doing something like that as adults—not dangerous exactly, yet I know it seemed so in Becky's eyes—somehow drew us closer.

We mentioned it between ourselves now and then as we grew older, recalling how much a seemingly beautiful moment had changed so suddenly, but also how it had turned out all right. Knowing that it was to be our final time alone together before Christopher's and my departure probably added to its seeming significance. That's why I wrote it down in detail in my journal.

CHAPTER 9

A SUDDEN SHOCK

Most of our things were packed away by the first of March.

Gradually a sort of solemn atmosphere began to settle over the house as the day of our departure drew nearer and nearer—fifteen days, then ten, then a week.

We were living out of two or three carpetbags by then, with four wooden crates containing the rest of our possessions all nailed together and sitting just inside the barn waiting to be loaded on a wagon and taken to the train in Miracle Springs. We would leave for Sacramento on March 16, three days before the ship was scheduled to sail from San Francisco.

I had done most of my crying by then. Now it was mostly sighs and conversations of pretended bravery. No one talked about the move anymore.

The sixteenth would come.

We would all go into town to the station together.

We would cry again.

Almeda and I would embrace, then Becky and I.

We would cry and blubber some more and talk about writing every day and about visiting next year, though in my heart I was so afraid I might never be back.

Pa and Christopher would exchange a handshake and a few manly words, during which Pa would tell Christopher to take good care of his daughter.

Then there would be handshakes from Zack and Tad.

Then I would hug Pa and my brothers too and would cry again, though the three of them would probably try not to.

Uncle Nick and Aunt Katie and all the younger kids would be there. Probably half the town would be there!

Then Christopher and I would get on the train, and as it pulled out we would wave to everyone through an open window. Everyone would be trying to smile and laugh as they waved, but what an empty feeling there would be in my stomach. Gradually the train would pick up steam, and we would pull out of Miracle Springs . . . and that would be that. Christopher and I would sit down in our seats in silence, and everybody else would walk quietly out of the station and back to whatever they had to do.

And life would go on.

I had envisioned the scene already in my mind a hundred times.

We didn't talk about it. The day was coming, and we would just do what must be done when the time came to do it.

By March 10, a Wednesday, I didn't think I could stand it another day. We would be leaving in less than a week and I wished we could just leave right then and get it over with. The hours crept by so slowly. The waiting was awful!

Then suddenly a shock wave slammed into our lives that changed everything.

The first evidence of it came that afternoon of the tenth when suddenly the sound of galloping hooves came pounding up the road. You could tell something was wrong just by the urgent sound of them.

Becky and I were talking together. We ran out of the bunkhouse about the same time Almeda appeared on the porch of the house with a look of concern on her face.

"Pa, Pa!" cried Zack as he flew up to the front of the house. "Where's Pa?"

"Up at your uncle's," replied Almeda, "—why, what's—"

But she could not even finish her question. Zack had already wheeled his horse around and was making for Uncle Nick's as fast as he could go.

"What is it?" I said as Becky and I ran up.

"I don't know," replied Almeda. "He wanted your father, that's all he said."

We were still standing there a couple minutes later when Zack again appeared, still galloping furiously. This time he didn't even slow down as he came but kept right on back in the direction of town. Before the sound of his horse was gone, Pa's feet sounded on the path as he came running down from Uncle Nick's as fast as I'd ever seen him go.

"Avery's had an attack!" he called, not even coming to the house, but running straight to the barn.

Almeda's hand went to her mouth as she gasped in shock.

"Oh, the dear man," she whispered. "God bless him."

For a second or two she and Becky and I stood there looking at each other in stunned silence. Then, as if we all suddenly realized the same thing at the same instant, we all tore off to the barn to hitch up a buggy.

Pa was off before we were done, just about the same time Uncle Nick came riding down from his place. He and Pa galloped off together toward town. Tad and Christopher had by now heard the commotion and had come running. Tad quickly saddled his horse, while Christopher gave us a hand with the buggy.

In a few minutes more Christopher and I, along with Becky, Almeda, and Ruth, were in the buggy, following about a minute behind Tad, with Aunt Katie and her family right behind us.

CHAPTER 10

PASSING ON OF A LEGACY

By the time we reached the Rutledge home, already several buggies and horses stood outside.

Christopher reined in the horse to a trot, then to a walk as we approached the house. Already a sense of eerie quiet was stealing over us.

Christopher parked the buggy and set the brake. We all got out quietly, suddenly becoming very aware of noise. We walked inside.

No one was in the living room. We continued toward the bedroom, tiptoeing as we crept forward. The door was open and we could hear a few subdued voices coming from inside.

Harriet Rutledge glanced up from the bedside as we entered. She rose and came toward us.

"Oh, Almeda . . . Corrie," she said, then was suddenly in both our arms together.

"Harriet," whispered Almeda tenderly, "I am so sorry. Is he . . ."

Harriet shook her head. "I don't know," she said, then began to cry softly.

Christopher walked past us toward the bed, where Doc Shoemaker and Pa and a few other men were gathered. Pa and Uncle Nick had arrived only a few minutes before us, and the doctor was trying to explain to them Rev. Rutledge's condition.

"He's had a stroke of paralysis," I heard him say in a subdued tone. "You never know exactly what part of the body these things will affect."

"Will he—" Pa said, letting the anxious expression of his face finish his question.

"Too soon to tell," replied the doc. "Usually if a man lives for twenty-four or forty-eight hours after an attack of this kind he's got a decent chance—but you never know what's going to happen."

"Ain't there something you can do, Doc?" asked Uncle Nick.

"Not a thing," sighed Doc Shoemaker, shaking his head slowly. "I wish there was, but I've got to wait just like everybody else."

Christopher listened to the brief conversation in silence. He probably knew better than anyone in the room that in a crisis such as this, his own profession, and that of the man lying motionless on the bed, was more required even than that of the physician in attendance.

Harriet and Almeda now approached the bed. I followed a step behind them. Almeda gently reached forward and took the limp white hand of her long-time friend. Tears rose in her eyes.

"The dear man!" she whispered again as she softly caressed the aging skin.

Christopher now began to pray aloud. Though no one had expected it exactly, it felt like the most natural thing in all the world. Some of the men's hats came down off their heads as he spoke.

"Dear Father," he said, *"great Physician, Healer, and Giver of life—we place our dear friend, your servant, Avery Rutledge, into your hands. Touch him in this moment, fill his limbs with your life. Heal him, dear Lord. Make him whole again."*

A few amens and sniffles sounded through the small bedroom. Harriet and Mary were both crying.

Almost as if Christopher's prayer had awakened him, Rev. Rutledge now opened his eyes about halfway. His head did not move, but I could see his eyes glance first in one direction, then another, taking in his closest loved ones gathered about his bed.

"Ah, all my friends here," he whispered softly, "come to help ease an old man's dying."

His voice sounded different and weak, and only half of his lips moved as he spoke, as if he were talking out of only one side of his mouth.

"Oh, Avery—please don't say such a thing," sobbed Harriet, sitting on the side of the bed and laying her head on his chest.

Rev. Rutledge struggled to lift one of his arms, but couldn't. Almeda saw it and now took the arm and helped him lift it the rest of the way, laying it around Harriet's shoulders. Tenderly his fingers moved up and down as if to comfort his wife.

"Don't worry, Harriet," Rev. Rutledge whispered. "I'm not afraid. I've had a good life . . . the Lord's been better to me than I deserve."

Harriet continued to weep softly with her head on his chest.

The minister glanced up, his head now turning slightly. His eyes fell on Pa.

"Drum Hollister," he said, speaking very slowly, "you've been a good friend all these years . . . the best kind of friend . . . kind of man who will speak the truth. I've been more thankful for you than you can know."

He lifted his hand slightly from Harriet's shoulder. Pa seemed to know what he meant and stooped forward. Gently Rev. Rutledge touched his forehead, as if blessing Pa one last time.

"Thank you, Drum . . . for being the man you are . . . and being my friend."

Pa gazed deeply into his eyes, then stepped back with a nod, a sniff, and a smile, unable to say a word. Tears were streaming down his face, but he hardly seemed to notice, and he did nothing to wipe them away.

Rev. Rutledge now spoke a few words to Uncle Nick, then to a few of the others. His voice was not strong but sounded deliberate. I could tell he was determined to say what he wanted to say, whatever the effort and no matter how long it took.

"Almeda," he said, turning toward the side of the bed where she and I stood beside Harriet, "my dear friend whose efforts brought me to California so many years ago . . . you will always hold a fond place in my heart. Thank you . . . for all you have meant to Harriet and me."

Almeda leaned forward, tears dripping from her eyes as she did, and lovingly kissed the minister on the forehead.

"Oh, and, Corrie," Rev. Rutledge now said to me, "you dear young lady—what joy you have brought to my life."

"Thank you," I said through my tears. I reached out, took his hand for just a moment, and gave it a gentle squeeze. Imperceptibly I felt him return it and knew it was his way of passing on his blessing to me.

He continued to glance about, and now his eyes fell on his own eight-year-old daughter.

"My dear, dear Mary," he said in the most tender voice imaginable. "I love you more than you can realize." He paused to take a shallow breath. "I want you to do something for me," he added after just a moment. "Will you?"

"Anything, Papa," said Mary.

"I want you to pray to our God to show you how much your father has loved you . . . will you do that?"

Mary nodded.

"And then I want you to remember," her father went on, "that I am not really your Father. God only gave me . . . gave me to you for a little while, to help you learn about your real Father. He . . . is my Father too—and the Father of all of us. So if you miss me when I am gone . . . you must remember that I am with your real Father . . . remember that he is a better Father than I could ever be. I shall be with him and I shall speak of you often to him . . . and you may trust him for everything, . . . for he is a good Father, and he loves you even more than I do . . . and that is a great deal indeed—for I love you very, very much."

By now we were all crying, though doing our best to do so quietly. But at these last words of her husband's to their daughter, Harriet again broke into sobs.

"Dear, dear Harriet," said the minister softly, patting her again as much as he was able, "how I have loved you! But do not grieve for me . . . for I am happy. Thank God that he allowed us . . . these wonderful years . . . these years together—"

A choking sound came to his voice.

Doc Shoemaker stepped forward.

"Christopher . . ." came Rev. Rutledge's voice again. He seemed to be looking around, and now his voice was so weak I could scarcely hear it. Christopher stepped forward and bent his face down toward the bed. "Christopher . . . you must—Chr . . ."

Again he paused, breathing heavily. He was laboring and could hardly get the words out.

" . . . you . . . must—Christopher . . . take . . . take care . . . of my people."

Christopher was nodding as he spoke.

Suddenly Rev. Rutledge's eyes opened wide and seemed to fill with light. His mouth opened as he struggled to raise himself off the pillows. The half of his mouth that he could move seemed trying to say something.

"Harriet!" he finally managed to exclaim in a whisper barely audible. "Harriet . . . it's—it's . . . do you see—"

But then just as suddenly his whole frame seemed to collapse. His mouth relaxed in a smile as he fell back into the bed. I looked up from his mouth to his eyes and saw that they were now closed, though the light that had been in them seemed to linger just a few moments longer upon his face.

I knew he was dead.

Avery Rutledge, the man we had known and loved, was now with his Lord.

CHAPTER 11

THE CALL

Christopher and I went over to the Rutledges the next morning to see if we could help Harriet with anything. Christopher said he would take care of the arrangements if she wanted. He went to see the undertaker, Mr. Olerude, and he and Harriet and Christopher scheduled the funeral for Saturday, just three days before we were to leave. Harriet asked Christopher to officiate and asked Pa to deliver the eulogy.

What neither Christopher nor I realized was that during this same time there were other talks and arrangements going on around the community that had nothing to do with the funeral. While we had been at the Rutledges and in town on Thursday morning, Mr. Shaw, Mrs. Bosely, Aunt Katie, and Mr. Harding all came to pay Pa and Almeda a visit. Christopher and I didn't know anything about it until that same evening, just after supper, when a large buggy pulled up in front of the house. Almeda, who had been expecting them, jumped up to answer the door. There stood the same two men and two women, along with Harriet Rutledge.

"We have visitors," announced Almeda, leading the five newcomers into the house.

Everybody greeted one another. The three ladies and two men all had expressions on their faces that should have made me suspicious, as should have the fact that Almeda had made two extra pies that day and had just begun to make a new and large pot of coffee a few minutes before their arrival. It was an odd assembly of visitors, too, and I don't know why I didn't recognize it imme-

diately as the committee, but I think my mind was still too pre-
occupied with Rev. Rutledge's death and our impending departure.

"Actually, we've come to see you, Christopher . . . Corrie," said
Mr. Shaw after everyone had taken a seat and Almeda had poured
coffee all around.

Christopher and I glanced at one another with bewildered expressions. My first thought was that the visit must have something
to do with our leaving. Christopher thought it had to do with preparations for the funeral. We were both wrong.

"We're here on church business," continued Mr. Shaw. "I know
a man's death is a time when you sometimes don't think about
much else. And meaning no disrespect to Avery, because everyone
in town loved him, and Harriet knows it," he said, glancing over
to where Harriet sat, "but as soon as we all got word that the Lord
had taken him, some of us on the church committee found ourselves thinking about what we ought to do, and we realized maybe
we didn't have a whole lot of time to deliberate on the matter."

He paused and glanced around at some of the other committee
members.

"I went out to see Katie last night," now said Mrs. Bosely,
"right after I heard about poor Avery. I mentioned the matter to
her, then the two of us went to see Patrick, and then on my way
home I stopped by the Hardings. And after we'd all talked about
it, we realized we had all found ourselves thinking the same thing."

Christopher and I still sat listening, having no more idea what
they were all talking about than when they'd begun.

"What they're trying to say," now put in Mr. Harding, "is that
the four of us got together this morning and came out to pay a visit
to your Pa, Corrie, and Almeda to ask them what they thought,
and then to Harriet this afternoon to consult with her. And the long
and the short of it is that we're here to ask you, Mr. Braxton, if
you'd consider taking Avery's place and becoming the new pastor
of the Miracle Springs church."

My heart skipped a beat when I heard the words. I could hardly
believe what I had just heard Mr. Harding say!

I glanced over at Pa, then Almeda. Both of them were grinning
and looking at me as if in delight to have been part of the secret.

I broke into a smile, then looked at Christopher. His face showed that he was just as stunned as I had been.

"I . . . I don't know what to say," he said haltingly. "This comes . . . as quite a surprise," he added, finally smiling, "as you might imagine. You all know that Corrie and I are planning to leave for the East in just five days."

"Believe me, we *do* know," laughed Aunt Katie. "That's why we acted so quickly, as Patrick said. We knew we had no time to lose."

"But . . . but we've already made our plans. We're all packed, and the tickets are bought and paid for."

"We realize that, Mr. Braxton," said Mr. Shaw. "The church is prepared to reimburse you for the tickets if you cannot get a refund."

"Oh no—that's not what I meant," said Christopher. "It's not the expenditure so much as the fact that I had made the decision to go based on what I thought was the Lord's leading. Now this suddenly casts everything into a new light. I'm just at a loss to know how to respond."

As they talked, I could hardly contain myself! It was with *great* difficulty that I sat there and didn't start blabbing away. But I knew the decision was between Christopher and the others . . . actually, it was between Christopher and the Lord.

"All we're asking is that you pray about it, Christopher," said Aunt Katie, "and ask the Lord if perhaps this is what he wants you to do."

"I can promise you I will do that," replied Christopher.

"Remember what you told me about circumstances on the way down to Dutch Flat," now put in Zack from across the room.

"Yes, you're right," smiled Christopher, glancing over at him. "I do remember. Why else do you think I'm suddenly so confused!"

Everyone else now joined him in laughter.

"What do *you* think about all this, Harriet?" Almeda now asked.

"I cannot think of anything that would delight me more," the minister's widow replied. "I don't want to say anything to sway you one way or the other, Christopher," she went on, "because of all things I know that Avery would want you to do the Lord's will. But I will tell you this, that ever since word came to us right after the first of the year that you two planned to leave Miracle Springs, Avery was concerned for the future of the church. Several times he said to me, 'I'm confused, Harriet. I don't know what the Lord is doing, because I always thought Christopher and Corrie would take over the church when I retired. It gave me a great feeling of peace to know the Lord was preparing them to follow my pastorate. I was so certain of it. Now I don't know what will become of the church when it is time for me to step down.' "

As she spoke, it was like listening to Rev. Rutledge talking to us again, and everyone became quiet and thoughtful.

"He knew his health was failing," Harriet continued. "We both knew a change was coming. Of course, we did not expect it to be quite so sudden—"

She stopped and glanced away momentarily, dabbing her eyes with a handkerchief.

"So you see, Christopher," she went on once she had composed herself, "knowing that your following him was Avery's heart's desire—well, you can see why nothing could please me more."

Christopher nodded. "I understand," he said softly. "You are very kind. So was Avery to place such confidence in me."

He drew in a deep breath and let it out slowly.

"But you are also right in what you say, that we must do whatever *the Lord* wills, not what any of us might ourselves want."

He rose from his chair.

"If you will all excuse me, I would like to go outside and have some time alone with the Lord before I say anything further."

He turned to go.

"There is just one other small request we have," interrupted Mr. Harding.

Christopher stopped and turned.

"As this has all happened so suddenly, and as you are not leaving until next week, well, whatever your decision, we were hoping you might take the pulpit for this Sunday."

Christopher smiled. "A reasonable enough request," he said.

"Let me just go have some time to myself, and then we can talk about it further."

He turned again and left the house.

Almeda rose and walked into the kitchen. "Pie anyone?" she announced. "Fresh baked today!"

Christopher returned about fifteen minutes later.

Everyone was talking gaily, even Harriet, enjoying pie and coffee. I was both jubilant and nervous and knew I was talking far too much and too excitedly, but I couldn't help it.

Christopher walked in. Everyone quieted and turned toward him.

"All right," he said, "I think I can tell you this much at present. I *will* preach on Sunday. And it just may be that it will be used by God to show us what his will is concerning the future. Perhaps you shall all hate my sermon and withdraw the request!"

Everyone laughed. "Little chance of that, son," said Pa.

"Well, in any event, I shall be happy to stand in Avery's shoes at least this once. I will hope, as well, to be able to give you my answer to the larger question you have posed."

CHAPTER 12

CHRISTOPHER'S HALF OF
THE DECISION

There were probably more people at Avery Rutledge's funeral that Saturday than had been together in one place in or around Miracle Springs . . . ever. Even for the church picnics.

People came from as far away as Marysville and Auburn. Harriet was so moved to see what an impact her husband had had in so many lives. Many who came were people she didn't even know.

The church seemed extra full the next morning too. I don't know it if was out of respect for the departed minister who had been responsible for building the church in the first place or from curiosity about what my husband was going to say.

The first part of the service went pretty much as usual, with Mr. Harding, Pa, and Mr. Shaw all sharing announcements and scripture readings and Almeda leading the hymns with Harriet at the pump organ. Finally it came time for the sermon. Mr. Shaw introduced Christopher.

"I don't suppose Christopher Braxton's a stranger to any of you by this time," he said, "although you also know he's been planning on leaving our town two days from now with his wife, our own dear Corrie who used to be a Hollister. Most of you know by now that the church committee—that's me and Katie Belle, Douglas Harding, and Agnes Bosely, along with Harriet Rutledge, who we made a new member just this week—we've all asked Christopher to stay on in Miracle Springs and be our new pastor. He hasn't said yes or no yet, only that he'd pray about it, which I reckon is all you can expect from any man, and that he'd try to give us his answer today. So I'm going to turn the rest of the service over to him, and he can say anything he wants to us."

Mr. Shaw sat down. Christopher got up from beside me, walked to the front of everyone, took his place behind the small lectern, and gazed out toward us a long time without saying anything. I was so nervous. It was March 14. We were supposed to leave on Tuesday, and now all of a sudden our future was completely up in the air again.

Everyone was watching him, curious about what might be coming. Most folks had gotten to know Christopher pretty well in the more than two years since he'd arrived in Miracle Springs. But the one side of him they didn't know much about was the preacher side. It didn't seem like there was anybody else in the community who *could* take Rev. Rutledge's place. Yet now that the committee had asked Christopher to, everybody was wondering what kind of preacher he actually was. He'd done the funeral yesterday, of course. Besides that, folks had seen him work with his hands, and they'd talked to him, and they knew that he was my husband and was a good man. Now they were about to see a whole different side of him, and so they were naturally curious.

So was I. Even I didn't know what Christopher was going to say.

"I know you are bound to be all ears," he finally began, "about what I am planning to say. You are no doubt wondering both about what my answer is going to be *and*, if I do say yes, about what kind of preacher I might make after you have been so used to our friend and brother Avery Rutledge for so many years. I am not certain I can satisfy you on that score today, because I am not really planning to preach a sermon. There are a number of things I feel I need to share with you before a decision is finally arrived at. Very personal things. I think you will see the reason for what I say in a few moments."

He paused and took in a deep breath.

"When your committee came to see me on Thursday, the evening after Avery's passing, asking me if I would consider becoming your new pastor, I said to them, as Patrick has told you, that I would think and pray about it. Under any other circumstances I would have added that I also needed to talk with my new wife, whom you all know far better than you know me."

Heads turned my way and I tried to keep from getting too red.

"But in this case I did not say that, because I realized—and I know Corrie would agree—that this was a decision I had to make myself . . . between myself and the Lord. The thought of leaving Miracle Springs has not been easy for Corrie. She has been wonderfully trusting, but that decision was mine, and therefore to change it will have to be mine too."

I couldn't help feeling a little bad inside, because after Christopher and I had our long talk about trust, I wished I had been *more* trusting. But I appreciated his words nonetheless.

"Well, I *have* prayed about it," Christopher continued, "and the answer I am going to give you this morning is that in all fairness to you I think you need to know me better before either you *or* I reach a final decision in this matter.

"Therefore, I am going to tell you about myself this morning. I am going to tell you how I came to be here in Miracle Springs. I am going to tell you what kind of person I am, what kind of dreams and goals I have. Most important, I am going to tell you where I came from, what kind of person I used to be, and why I dedicated my life to the ministry in the first place. I feel it is important that you know me this well. I want you to know what you would be getting for your money, so to speak—although I would take no salary as your minister even if you do decide to continue your invitation to me.

"I am grateful to God for what he has done in me, yet in many respects I have had a difficult life. I feel it is imperative that you know of my background in some detail. I do not believe in the old horse dealer's adage that says let the buyer beware. If there is something wrong with the horse, it is incumbent upon the seller—if he is a Christian—to make that fact known to the buyer before the transaction is made. 'Let the buyer beware' is but another way of saying that you may deceive anyone you want, as long as he doesn't find out until it is too late for him to do anything about it—hardly a virtuous creed by which to live.

"I live by a different creed, one where openness and honesty and forthright integrity are at the top of the list. In honesty, therefore, I am bound to tell you that there are a few things wrong with this lame nag who is standing in front of you today—if I may prolong the equine parallel probably longer than is beneficial!—and whom you are considering employing to shepherd this small Miracle Springs church. I would be remiss if I did not point out these flaws and then allow you to reconsider your decision."

Christopher paused to take in a breath. A few chuckles went about the room from his comparing himself to a lame nag of a horse, but the illustration did relax everybody, and now they sat back in their seats to listen.

"In other words, I am perhaps not all I seem at first glance," Christopher went on. "I would have you know me, and know me well, before any final decision is reached. You may learn more about me and decide this is not the kind of man you want as your pastor, and I want that option to be plainly in front of you. I will not accept your call simply on the basis of the committee's kind offer. I would only accept if a majority of the church, after knowing me better, agreed that they were comfortable and happy with the selection."

My heart was pounding as I listened. Christopher sounded as if he might take the position! As if reading my mind, his next words resolved that part of the question.

"So *my* half of the answer to your gracious request, Mr. Shaw," he said, looking at Patrick Shaw as he spoke, "and you others of the committee—Katie, Douglas, Mrs. Bosely, and of course you, Harriet—" he said, glancing toward each of the others one at a time, "is this—that if the church wants us, *after* you hear my story this morning and have a chance to weigh its implications, then Corrie and I will remain in Miracle Springs, and I will become your pastor . . . and Corrie and I will *together* seek to serve and minister among you."

CHAPTER 13

CHRISTOPHER'S STORY

The words were no longer out of Christopher's mouth before a shriek of happiness sounded, and suddenly I realized it had come from *my* mouth!

I jumped out of my seat and ran up to Christopher and threw my arms around him, right there in front of everyone, while he watched in astonishment. What kind of undignified behavior was this, he must have thought, from the young lady who might well become the next minister's wife? But I couldn't help it.

"Oh, Christopher," I whispered in his ear, "I did trust you, and I do trust you . . . and I will be content to be with you wherever you go . . . oh, but I am so happy, I can't deny it!"

I took my arms from around him and turned around. Suddenly it dawned on me what I had done. There was the whole church looking at us and clapping, my own family most of all. I felt my face getting ten shades of red all at once, and I hurried back to my seat amid laughter which now mingled in with the applause.

"Perhaps you may find my *wife* the unsuitable half of this arrangement!" said Christopher.

Now everyone did laugh, including Christopher. Gradually the commotion settled down. Christopher waited until quiet had again descended, then took a deep breath and started in.

"The man you see before you and whom you know as Christopher Braxton," he began, "is much different from the Christopher Braxton who grew up in the farming regions of the Ohio valley."

He paused momentarily. "The big problem I had when I was growing up," he went on, "was simply that I did not feel that I was any good, or that I ever could be any good or could amount to anything. The memory of that feeling still lives with me and cannot help but affect the man I am today. These memories sometimes affect my confidence and weigh me down with inner burdens of insufficiency, even after all these years. I do not think I exaggerate," he added, "when I say that scars remain upon my soul from those years which will probably be permanent in this life. And it is because of these scars that I compared myself to a lame nag a few moments ago."

He paused and smiled lightly, though, I thought, a little sadly too.

"I would like to tell you briefly how these scars came to be on my soul, because if you take me, I'm afraid the scars come too, as part of the package that makes up the man called Christopher Braxton."

He stopped again and breathed in deeply, then began his story in earnest.

"My father was married twice," Christopher said. "I was a son of his second marriage. By his first marriage he had a number of children, but then his wife was killed in an accident. Some time later he married my mother, who was seventeen years younger than he. My father was a great deal older than me, and thus I never knew him well.

"My father was of Hutterite German, or Anabaptist descent. He spoke a form of the German language known as *high* German. The name Braxton, of course, is not German. Originally we were known by the name Brandeis, but my grandfather changed it when he emigrated to the United States. My mother was of north German extraction and spoke a dialect known as *low* German. But the difference between my father's people and my mother's was more than that of language. The closest parallel I can make in our own country of this distinction would be the social and prejudicial division between black and white.

"We lived in a mostly Hutterite community, where my mother was considered an outsider—almost like a Negro living in an all-white community. The Hutterites looked down on the 'low' Germans in exactly the same way many whites look down on Negroes or Indians, and my father rarely visited with our relatives on my mother's side of the family because—at least so it seemed to me as a young boy—they were viewed as inferior. My father only wanted us to visit with his Hutterite relatives. Why he married my mother in the first place is a bit of a puzzle in my mind. But he did marry her, and this was the situation when my earliest memories begin to gather themselves in the distant regions of my brain.

"But it was really no advantage to visit our relatives on my father's side of the family either. When we saw them, all the relatives treated myself and my four brothers and sisters like dirt. We were a family, as it were, caught between the two worlds of *high* and *low*—outcasts really, not accepted by either, and looked down upon by both. Throughout my early years I continually heard things like 'You're no good, Chrissy.' Therefore I grew up with that feeling that I was worth nothing as a human being. I knew I was a second- or even a third-class citizen.

"The one bright spot in my life was school. I didn't necessarily get treated any better there because we lived in a Hutterite community. But I loved learning. Books and stories were like treasures to me. They offered me a way to escape my pain.

"If anyone had said to me in those days, 'Someday you will be the pastor of a church . . . there will be people you will speak to . . . you will teach and help them . . . you will counsel and marry them . . . you will stand in front of large groups of men and women,' I would have laughed at the impossibility of the very idea. The thought that I might someday do something—*anything!*—worthwhile was incredible to me. What could I—little Chrissy Braxton—possibly be but a complete failure?"

Even though I had heard the story before, it was still difficult for me to imagine Christopher as feeling worthless. From the moment I met him, he had seemed so inwardly strong and so sure of himself. If it hadn't been for him, I would not even be alive right now. The thought of our first meeting sent my mind back to those first days when I'd awakened on Mrs. Timms' farm in Virginia after my injury. Even now I could see, in my mind, that strong yet tender face looking down at me—the same face I saw now behind the pulpit of my church.

"My father was in his late sixties by the time I entered my teen years," Christopher was now saying. "He had been a good man early in life, even a godly man whom many people looked up to. But besides losing a wife, he had lost a great deal of money when a depression hit. So by the time we children of his second family came along, he was aging and feeling many frustrations. He was beginning to show signs of mental infirmity, and from time to time he really treated us badly. When we misbehaved, even for some minor offense, he grabbed us by the hair and hit us with his hand. I was a timid and self-conscious boy, and the fear this caused within me was devastating. There is no other way to say it—I was terrified of him, even though, as I say, he was not by nature a cruel man.

"So I did not have the experience of a warm and loving and personal father. At that point in my life, if someone had told me, in trying to communicate God's great love and goodness, that he was my Father and loved me like a Father, my response would have been to stare in bewilderment. If God was like a *father*—as I envisioned the word—why would I want to have anything to do with him?

"When I was fourteen, after an illness of about a year, my mother died. She was only fifty years old at the time, and there were still four of us children at home. At the age of fourteen, I watched my own mother die, and let me tell you—I was not prepared for that. If any family needed a mother, ours certainly did.

"The very night of my mother's death, at one o'clock in the morning, knowing that my father, now approaching seventy, could not possibly take care of us children, our high German relatives from his side of the family came in and broke up our home. My brother went to an older married sister, I went to a half brother by my father's previous marriage, my younger brother went to an aunt, and my younger sister went to a different aunt. My poor younger sister spent the next years moving around from relative to relative and suffered far more than even I did.

"In any event, I lost my mother and my immediate family all in the same day. These changes came at such a critical time in my growing young life, when I already thought of myself as worthless. You can imagine how much deeper the wounds that were already there *now* went within me. As I said, I went to live with an older half brother and his wife, and I knew they didn't want me."

I felt tears creeping up into my eyes as Christopher related his story. So much of what he'd told me those first days and weeks at Mrs. Timms' about his struggles in his church had taken on even deeper meaning as I learned about his early life in more detail. How much more painful it must have been for him than I realized at the time.

Christopher's words came back to me about his ouster from the Richmond church: *The following days and weeks were of such anguish and loss. My brain and heart were singed as with a scorching fire, and there suddenly seemed nothing left to live for. Everything I cared about had been swept away as by a hot desert wind—leaving nothing but the dry sands of the Sahara in its place. I felt worse than empty—emptier than empty. I felt a void, a nothingness, a hot parching thirst but with no water to drink, no water anywhere.*

Now as he described the loss of his mother, I saw how terrible the loneliness from yet another rejection must have been for him.

"My half brother and his wife," Christopher went on, "kept me for two years. One day my sister-in-law came and bluntly said to me, 'You're sixteen now. We can't keep you here any longer. You're going to have to find someplace else to live. You're too old to go to school anymore. You need to find work and make your own way.'

"I was devastated. I knew nobody. I had no place to go. I'd never thought much about what I'd do when I couldn't go to school anymore. I didn't know *what* to do. Desperation grew in me. I knew they wanted to get rid of me . . . but I didn't know where I could go.

"The summer came and I knew I had to leave. What a terrible feeling it is not to be wanted—to know that no one on the face of the earth wants you. That's how I felt. Finally, it occurred to me that perhaps someone on my mother's side, the low German side, of the family *might* receive me better than those on my father's. All through the years, *both* sides of the family had treated us like outcasts. But I hoped, with my father and mother both dead, that my mother's relatives might feel a little more sympathy for my plight.

"So one day early in the summer I packed up all my earthly possessions, which only amounted to a few clothes and a book or two, in a case held together with string. I said my goodbyes to my half brother's family, though none of them revealed the least display of love or emotion at my leaving. Then I walked out the door, having no idea toward what kind of future my feet would lead me.

"I set out walking to the town of Willard, which was twelve or fifteen miles away. I'd probably walked a mile or two when a man in a farm wagon, pulled by two tired-looking horses, came up from behind and asked me if I would like a ride.

" 'Thank you!' I said, and jumped up beside him.

"I was glad for the ride. Once we were on our way, however, the fellow looked over at me with a gruff expression.

" 'Where you going, kid?' he asked.

" 'Willard,' I answered cautiously. My voice was scratchy and high because it hadn't completely changed to a man's voice yet. I was really young. Even though I was sixteen, I probably looked twelve and was so timid I was afraid of my own shadow.

" 'What you aimin' to do in Willard, boy?' the man shot back in a deep, angry-sounding voice. My spirit was already crushed. I was as worried as I could be, because I didn't *know* what I was going to do in Willard. Just the sound of the man's voice made me quake in my thin boots that hardly had any leather left on their soles.

" 'I . . . uh, figured to get work in the fields,' my high-pitched little voice answered.

" 'Willard's a tough place, kid,' he said. ''Sides, you're a mite on the scrawny side to get work in the fields. You ain't gonna get no work in Willard nohow!'

"I can still feel the hot tears as they began to burn out of my eyes at the man's words. I glanced away and said nothing more.

"After a while the man spoke up again.

" 'Where you wanna go in Willard?'

" 'My grandmother's house,' I answered, not daring to look over at him.

" 'Where does she live?'

" 'I don't know,' I said.

" 'How you expect to get there if you don't know where she lives?'

" 'I . . . I was there when I was younger,' I said. 'I figured if I got to Willard, I . . . I'd be able to find it.'

"The answer seemed to satisfy him for the moment, and he said nothing more.

"I rode all the way to Willard with him, mostly in silence, my fear and uncertainty over my future mounting with every mile. As we finally rode into the small town two or three hours later, suddenly I saw a house I recognized as my grandmother's.

" 'Hey . . . there it is,' I said. 'That's my grandmother's house!'

"The man stopped his wagon. I grabbed my case and jumped down.

" 'Thanks for the ride, mister,' I said.

"I walked over to the house, timidly climbed up the steps, knocked on the door, and waited. My mother's sister, Aunt Mary, an unmarried schoolteacher who still lived with my grandmother, came to the porch. She looked through the screen door hesitantly, then slowly opened it.

" 'Chrissy,' she exclaimed, calling me by the nickname my relatives had always used. Whenever I heard it I felt they were making fun of me. Now I was sixteen and still being called a little girl's name. 'What are *you* doing here?' she said. There was no hint of welcome or tenderness in her tone.

" 'They . . . they made me leave where I was,' I half stammered. 'I . . . I got no place else to go.'

"Aunt Mary looked me over a few long seconds in silence.

" 'Well, I'll go call Grandma,' she sighed with notable reluctance, then turned and left me standing there.

"Next, Grandma came to the door. She asked the same question—what was I doing there?—her voice containing even greater annoyance than my aunt's. I repeated my story.

" 'I'm trying to find a job,' I said, 'and . . . I need someplace to stay.'

"She thought for a minute. 'You'd best get yourself into town then,' she said, 'where the farmers gather. Ask around. See if there's anyone needing a hired boy.'

"By now I was really hungry. I'd been up since four in the morning, and I hadn't had anything to eat all that time. But I didn't dare ask for anything. So I just turned and did what Grandma said and wandered off in the direction of town.

"I spent the rest of the morning knocking on the door of every farmhouse, asking everyone I saw about work. But it was no use. I was just a skinny kid with a high voice, and nobody needed the likes of me. At the grain mill I joined a group of men waiting to be picked by some farmers for work in the fields. Every man there was eventually picked but me. As the men began leaving in wagons, I hid behind a shed so no one would see me standing there alone.

"Finally I walked dejectedly back to my grandmother's. I was afraid to go knock on the door again. I knew they didn't want me there. That fact was obvious enough from their looks and sighs and tones. But I had nowhere else. I literally had no place to call home.

"So I walked around to the back porch and sat down, hoping in time that either my grandmother or my aunt would notice me and invite me in. Finally I heard the screen door open behind me.

" 'What did you find out, Chrissy?' asked my aunt. I told her I hadn't found out anything. She turned without another word and went back inside.

"A little while later my grandmother came out. She asked the same question. I gave her the same answer. Then she turned and went back inside.

"I kept sitting there. I didn't know what to do. I was so hungry I was beginning to get dizzy from the heat. Then, to my horror, I heard the clinking of silverware and dishes inside. I realized my aunt and grandmother were eating lunch!

"The sound of it was too awful to bear.

"I couldn't stand to listen to the sounds of them eating. I got up from the porch and walked back around to the front of the house, lay down under a big shade tree, and finally cried myself to sleep."

Christopher stopped and looked down, blinking hard and sniffing a few times. He pulled out his handkerchief and blew his nose. The church was still as could be. I could hardly look at him without bursting into tears myself. I was weeping just to listen, but I tried hard not to make any noise. I wanted to run right up in front of the church and throw my arms around him. It was so quiet. Everyone felt for him having to relive such sad and lonely memories.

"Several hours later," he went on, "my aunt came out, saw me lying there, and woke me up. I suppose she and Grandma had realized that if it got much later I'd still be hanging around by evening, and then they'd have no choice but to take me in.

" 'You want to go see Amos?' she asked, referring to my younger brother, who at the time was living with some relatives about five miles away.

"I nodded. I scarcely paused to think that this was their way of getting rid of me—*anything* would be better than this, I thought.

"Aunt Mary hitched up the wagon and drove me the five miles. Later that evening I was taken to yet another aunt's house, who finally told me, since there was no place else, that if I could find a job I could stay there with her family.

"Well, there is no need to recount every detail of this part of my life except to say that by my late teen years I was crushed to a pulp. I managed to find work here and there. God took care of me, but those were very, very hard times. Over and over I was told that I wasn't ever going to amount to anything. Not only did my relatives seem to feel no need to display any compassion, they also seemed to consider it their duty to remind me over and over how worthless I was, which they lost no opportunity to do. This is something about the human species I have never understood, and still do not understand—why there seems an inborn compelling to ridicule and hurt and make fun of those less fortunate than ourselves.

"In all honesty, I must confess that I could not help being angry at the relatives on my father's side. There had been a great deal of money in the family at one time. Many of my half brothers and sisters and aunts and uncles owned nice large farms. Yet no one lifted a finger to help me or my brothers and sisters. Those on my mother's side showed no more compassion, as is clear enough from my first hours in Willard. My aunt at least let me stay with her, and for a couple of years I managed to find enough work here and there to pay her for my board and room.

"I mention this anger to show that spiritually, during these years of my late teens, what was growing within me was not faith, but resentment. When you are very young, all you do is hurt, without thinking about *why*. As you grow, however, you begin to wonder why *you* have been singled out for such hardships. The minute you begin asking that question, frustration and bitterness—and usually anger—set in.

"This anger that I felt toward my relatives as the years passed I gradually transferred to God, as many people do. I thought that God had altogether forgotten me and did not care any more about me than anyone ever had. I was worthless in everyone else's eyes . . . I figured I was worthless in God's eyes too.

"Sometime during these years, therefore, I determined that I was not going to believe in God anymore. Thus, I declared myself an atheist. What had God ever done for me? I thought. Why should I bother about him?

"I had an older brother, however, who had had just about as tough a time of it as I had and had felt the same rejections from the relatives. Joe had struck out on his own quite a while before and was now married and living down in Mansfield. More important, he had become a Christian. When I was eighteen I went to visit him, hoping he might be able to help me get a job.

"So I went to my brother, and he saw in an instant that I needed help, emotionally, spiritually, and every other way.

" 'You know what would be good for you, Chris?' Joe said, '—school . . . maybe even a Bible college.'

" 'Bible college?' I replied. 'But I'm an atheist.'

" 'God loves atheists just as much as Christians,' Joe replied with a smile.

"I didn't have an answer for that one!

"But I loved to read and learn. Secretly, in fact, I had harbored a dream of going to college someday. Of course I never saw any way such a thing would ever be possible. My brother's bringing up the subject suddenly brought the dream to life.

" 'But I've got no money,' I said. 'How could I ever afford to go to school? Besides, I'm not interested in going to college to study the Bible.'

"Not only was my brother a Christian, he had attended a Bible college in Richmond, Virginia, for two years himself. And now came the surprise.

" 'Tell you what, Chris,' he said, 'if you will agree to attend the Richmond Bible Institute, *I'll* back you up to make sure you don't get into any financial difficulties.'

"I could not believe my ears.

"My brother *believed in me* enough to make such an offer! It was a shocking thought. The wheels of my mind quickly began to turn. His offer would give me a whole year to find work. If I could work along with my studies, I could begin saving money for future years . . . and *continue* going to college!

"Even though I still believed myself to be an atheist, this Bible college would give me a chance to realize my dream of obtaining a higher education. Though I did not know it at the time, God really did have my life in his hands.

"Of course I agreed to my brother's proposal.

"Over the course of the next few years, after I traveled down to Richmond, life gradually began to look up for me. I met people in the city who *accepted* me, not because I was or was not a Hutterite or anything else . . . *but just because of who I was.*

"You cannot imagine what that was like for a young man who had never experienced full and unconditional acceptance in his life."

Sitting in that pew and listening to Christopher talk, I again found myself thinking of things he had told me right after our meeting, this time about his desire to tell people of God's love. Now I saw that desire from a larger perspective: *I found growing within me an enormous hunger to help people be complete. To help them become full people, to help them know their heavenly Father intimately and wonderfully, to help them to see and know God and be his sons and daughters, to know that he was not a faraway God Almighty and Omnipotent somewhere in the distant heavens, but that he was a close and present and tender and compassionate and loving Father to them. And it was this hunger that led me toward the ministry.*

"I cannot point to a day or an hour when I suddenly *believed* in God again," he was telling the congregation. "I suppose perhaps, in a way, I never really stopped believing in him. When I speak of 'believing' in him again, maybe what I mean is when I was able to *admit* to myself that I believed in him.

"The process was gradual. But as I read and studied and interacted with people at the school, studying not just the Bible but all the disciplines of learning, over the course of time I gradually knew that I *did* believe and had really believed all along. As I matured, I came to recognize that God had been watching out for me and protecting me and nurturing me all through the years of pain and inner conflict over my worth. The acceptance I began to feel from others, I began to feel from him too.

"Not only did I come to realize that God accepted me, I began to realize that he *loved* me—in an active way, not merely passively, that he loved me energetically and had purposes for me which I could step into and be part of.

"What a change this was!

"It meant I was a person who mattered! I wasn't a nothing as I'd thought all those years. I was *somebody* . . . because I was God's son. I was actually *worth* something.

"God began—I can think of no other way of describing it—to reveal to me just what it meant that Jesus continually called him *Father* and told us to do likewise. I struggled and struggled with memories of my own imperfect father, trying to come to grips with why God had chosen such a flawed human relationship—that between fathers and their sons and daughters—to describe his relationship with the men and women he had created.

"This was a great internal battle for me," said Christopher. "The mere word *father* conjured up images and emotions of hurt. The phrase *God is a loving Father* set up an oxymoronic dichotomy in my mind that I could not resolve. The concepts *love* and *fatherhood* did not go together."

As Christopher spoke, I remembered the struggle I had had too with anger against Pa when we had first come to California, feeling like he'd run out on us. I'd had to learn how *father* and *love* could go together too, just like Christopher was describing.

"Yet once I began to see God's Fatherhood with clarity," Christopher went on, "I also began to see earthly fatherhood from a more proper perspective as well. Perhaps the time may come when I will have the opportunity to tell you in more detail what I believe God showed me in this way. But for now, suffice it to say that for the first time I began looking up into God's face and trying to call him *Father*, knowing that he loved me, and then asking him what kind of man he wanted me to be.

"I say *try* because it was extremely difficult at first. I called God *Father* out of obedience to Jesus, who told us to address him in this way. Even the word *Father* was difficult to say in my prayers. I literally could not pray to God that way. Yet gradually I got more and more used to it. And of course I need hardly say that forgiveness occupied a great deal of this gradual process. As I learned to say *Father* to God, I found more and more forgiveness welling up within me for my own earthly father, and then, surprisingly enough, for all the others toward whom I had allowed bitterness to fester within my heart.

"You cannot imagine how transforming this process was, so much so that I began to hunger to share this wonderful newfound love with others who, perhaps like myself, did not know that God was a *good* Father who cared about them. If God could love *me* and pull *me* out of the hole of worthlessness in which I had lived most of my life, then he could do so for *anyone*! And perhaps I could help people to know what I had not known during my boyhood—that they were valuable in God's sight.

"The more I thought and prayed and studied, the more I realized that every single human being is important in God's sight. I hungered to tell this to people who, like myself for so many years, did not know that wonderful truth. I wanted to tell it to unbelievers and non-Christians. I hungered even more to help people in churches, God's people, grow to know their Father more intimately.

"God created us as special individuals. He loves each one of us so much. How enormous these truths were for me! I had felt such rejection that when I realized I was a special and unique individual in God's sight—*everything* changed.

"A great passion grew within me to help people become complete men and women—to point their eyes toward God, even when all else in life seemed discouraging and without hope. I wanted people to become sons and daughters of their very personal Father. And this was what ultimately got me thinking about the ministry. I never aspired to having letters after my name, only to be used by God."

Christopher paused, then smiled.

"I told you at the beginning," he said, "that I wanted to share with you not only my past, but also of my goals and dreams and why I entered the ministry in the first place. And this I have just said goes a long way to clarify those things. But let me continue with the rest of the background story.

"There were two parts of the Bible school—a regular college where, in addition to Bible and religion courses, all the standard academic disciplines were taught, and a seminary for the specific training of ministers. Regular college degrees were given, as well as divinity degrees.

"After two years in the regular college, I applied for the divinity program. I was twenty-one at the time. This seemed the most likely way to tell people what I now knew about God. It seemed to me that the best avenue through which to help people as I wanted to do would be as the pastor of a church. It seemed that in the church I could do the most good in helping people come to know their heavenly Father.

"I was accepted into the program. This now became my goal—to obtain a Doctor of Divinity degree and to enter the ministry. Since I did not yet have a college degree, the school allowed me to continue my studies at both the college and the seminary concurrently. Many of the classes were night classes, and thus I was able to work half days in order to support myself.

"My body had continued growing longer than for most young men, and even in time a bit of muscle began to appear on my once-scrawny frame. By the time I had moved from Ohio down to Richmond two years prior to this, I was able to get jobs fairly easily. Therefore, I worked my way through college and seminary at a granary, hoisting around hundred-pound bags of wheat. So I never actually needed the financial help my brother had offered. Yet his offer at the time had been what had made the difference in my decision.

"I graduated when I was twenty-five and then spent more than two years as pastor of a sizable church there in the city of Richmond, Virginia, which is where I happened to be when the war broke out. My stand on the war, however, fell uncomfortably upon the ears of the leaders of my congregation. My resignation was requested. That rejection caused my doubts and questions about myself to resurface—though never again did I question the love of God the Father.

"From that time until my leaving the East for Miracle Springs,

I worked as foreman and caretaker of a small farm outside the city, which is where I was working when the Lord smiled upon me and brought your own Corrie Belle Hollister—as she was then—into my life."

Christopher paused, let out a breath that seemed to say he was relieved to have everything said, and looked around the room.

"Well, my friends, there you have a brief capsule of my life's story to this point. I do not know if that will help you with your decision, but I feel more comfortable in the realization that you now know these things about me."

CHAPTER 14

THE ANSWER

It was such a moving testimony that most of the women, and even some of the men, had tears in their eyes as they listened. Mr. Shaw stood up as soon as Christopher had finished his final prayer and walked to the front.

"I propose we put the matter to a vote before the whole church right now," he said.

"Then you will not mind if I excuse myself," said Christopher. "I would not have your discussion hampered by my presence."

I rose to join him, and we walked down the aisle and outside, everyone smiling up at us from their seats as we passed.

"Oh, Christopher," I said as soon as we were outside, "all I can think of is how sad it must have been for you after your mother died. I feel the same way whenever I hear that part of your story."

"The Lord has a story for all our lives to tell," he replied, "and every good story has its sad times, otherwise the happy parts wouldn't be as wonderful."

He smiled tenderly at me, and I could see what he meant right in his face. Christopher became very quiet as we walked slowly away from the church.

"I'm so proud of you," I said.

"I'm afraid it was far too long," he sighed.

"You said you wanted them to know Christopher Braxton all the way to the bottom. Now they do."

"But I should perhaps have spread it out over a couple of weeks."

"We don't have two weeks. Besides, you told me once that if you ever had the chance to preach again you would tell people enough beforehand either to nail your coffin shut or welcome your ministry with open arms. I would say you did just that."

"I always become self-conscious after I have spent myself with a lengthy outpouring."

"Self-conscious? That's not how you sounded to me. You sounded sure of every word."

"I am sure when I am speaking about who God is and what he does. But then often that little boy jumps back to the front—the little fellow I told them about in there, timid and fearful and convinced no one cares for anything he has to say."

"But that little fellow is just going to have to realize that he is a man now—a strong man, one of God's men—and that people *want* to hear what he has to say."

Christopher sighed again. "I'll try to remember," he said, smiling back to me.

"So, Mrs. Braxton," he said after a moment's pause, now trying to sound cheerful, "what do you think of the prospect of being a minister's wife?"

"It is certainly a new twist to this new life we've started," I replied, trying to laugh away my lingering sadness. "And not one I expected!"

"You knew what you were getting when you married me . . . didn't you?"

"I don't suppose I ever thought through what it would mean to *me* if the offer of a church did come along. Even though all this time since we decided to go east you have been talking about the ministry, the thought of being a *minister's wife* hadn't really sunk in."

"Does it frighten you?"

"I don't think so. I suppose I'm a little apprehensive. What woman wouldn't be? What if I don't measure up to people's expectations? Most of these people still think of me as a little girl. But the prospect of being here in Miracle Springs outweighs all those fears."

"I want you to be as free of doubts about this—if we *do* stay, and if it turns out they want us—as are the people in the church," he said, motioning back behind us.

"I want you to be where God wants you to be," I said, "serving him among people as I know your heart yearns to do. Of course I want to stay here. But most important of all is the fact that you are my husband, Christopher. Where you go, I will go. What you do, I will do. You are the head of this marriage. I want you to be happy and fulfilled. That's what will make *me* happy. If it is in the East, I will be thankful, if here in Miracle Springs, I will be thankful. What do *you* think—do you *want* to accept the invitation here?"

"I can honestly say that I could be happy and content either way. Of course, the thought of having a position from which to minister to a wide range of people and to be able to communicate God's truths—the thought of it is wonderful. We might go to the East and have no such opportunity present itself. And now, here *is* such an opportunity right in front of us. Who can deny that it appears to be God's leading? Yet truthfully, Corrie, the ambition toward the pastorate was burned out of me during the years of my pruning at the Lord's hand while at Mrs. Timms' farm. My desire to go east was not born out of ambition, only ministry, and here it seems to be right in Miracle Springs. I want only what God wants, and nothing more. If that means for you and me to take the Rutledges' place as the ministers of the Miracle Springs church, then I will rejoice. What *he* wants will be best. *That* is what I want."

Before I could say another word, we heard voices. Turning back, we saw people coming out of the church.

"Didn't take them long, did it?" said Christopher.

As Pa and Almeda came out and down the steps, I saw them speak to Tad, Becky, Zack, and Ruth, then the three older ones fell in step behind them, while Almeda took Ruth's hand. Their faces were very serious.

Oh no! I thought, my heart suddenly sinking, *Pa was telling them not to say anything and let him be the one to break the bad news!* I don't know what I would think myself, but I couldn't stand it for Christopher if the church voted against him!

They walked toward us. I couldn't tell a thing from anyone's face. They looked pretty somber.

I finally couldn't wait any longer!

"Pa!" I said in exasperation.

He glanced up, still with a blank expression, as if he didn't have a notion what I could mean.

"*Pa* . . . what did they say?" I exclaimed.

"About what?"

"You know! Do they want us or not?"

Slowly now Pa's face broke into a grin.

" 'Course they want you," he said, then stuck out his hand to Christopher. "Congratulations, son . . . or should I say Rev. Braxton?"

They shook hands, and then everyone else gathered around us, all talking at once.

"No Reverend, please," said Christopher with a sigh of thankful relief. "With all due respect to your late minister, it is a title I am not altogether comfortable with. I will be no different as a pastor than as a layman, and *Christopher* will suit me just fine for both roles."

"They really want Christopher to be the minister?" I asked excitedly. "Why did you all come out of there with such long faces?"

"I thought I'd make you sweat a little," laughed Pa.

"Oh, Pa . . . how could you do it?"

"Yes, they want you," said Almeda. "Harriet stood up the instant you were gone and said that she knew beyond any doubt that God had sent you to Miracle Springs to replace her husband. She said she knew Avery would be wonderfully pleased."

"A few of them said Christopher might be a little radical," said Tad.

"But then others said some radical religion might be good for 'em," added Zack.

"Everyone thinks this is quite a young man you found for yourself, Corrie," said Almeda.

"I agree," I added, looking up into Christopher's face.

He was smiling now. I was so happy for him!

"Well, come on," said Pa. "They told us to bring you back in."

We turned and followed him back up the steps into the church. Mr. Shaw was at the door with a big smile on his face, his hand outstretched.

"The vote was unanimous!" he said, shaking Christopher's hand.

"Come on back inside—both of you," Mr. Shaw was saying. "The congregation wants to greet its new pastor."

Christopher smiled and took my hand, and we walked back into the church. The moment we appeared, for the second time that day, everyone broke into applause, and now rose to go. We stood at the back of the church near the door and greeted everyone on their way outside. Christopher made sure Harriet Rutledge shared the greeting time with us. That reminded me of the sad fact that her husband was so soon gone, which was the only reason all this was happening. We stood on one side of the door and she on the other.

It took forever for the church to empty out.

They all wanted to speak personally to the three of us, telling Harriet how much they had loved Rev. Rutledge and expressing their condolences and at the same time telling Christopher and me how glad they were that we were going to be the new minister and minister's wife of Miracle Springs.

In between handshakes, just after Mrs. Sinclair and Mrs. Gilly had both said very nearly that same thing, he bent down and whispered laughing in my ear, "I wonder what they'll say about us when they get away from the church!"

Even the banker Mr. Royce seemed moved. The only time I'd ever seen that man show any sensitive emotion at all was when he'd come over to our house for Christmas dinner several years back. But on this day, as he shook hands with Christopher on the way out of church, I could tell that what had been said had gone even deeper inside him. He clutched Christopher's hand longer than usual and just stared at him deeply in the eyes as if he was trying to say something. But he couldn't get any words out. Finally he gave Christopher's hand another shake, mouthed the two words *Thank you* without hardly any sound to them, then hurried off down the steps and to his carriage without a word to anyone.

Even after the enthusiastic vote, the church committee wanted to make the affirmation of their call to Christopher official. They came to the house that same afternoon, about an hour later, said they'd met again, considered everything both Christopher and the congregation had said, and wanted him to know that the call was unanimous and official, then handed him a written letter of invitation containing each of their four signatures, as well as Harriet's.

Christopher thanked them. "But I still intend to give you one final opportunity to change your minds," he added, "before I shall give you my final answer. I said earlier that I wanted you to hear my story *and* have the chance to weigh its implications."

"Are we to take that to mean, Mr. Braxton," asked Mr. Harding, somewhat confused by Christopher's words, "that you will or will not occupy the pulpit this evening?"

"I will be happy to conduct this evening's service," Christopher replied.

"Well, be assured, Mr. Braxton, that the whole church is behind you."

"Thank you. I appreciate that very much. But I will reserve further comment until after this evening's service, when you shall have the opportunity I mentioned."

They all shook hands, then the committee turned and left, three of them in Mr. Harding's carriage, and Aunt Katie by foot. As we watched them go, Christopher slipped his arm around my waist. We stood side by side gazing down the road until they were out of sight.

"What did you mean," I asked, "by saying you wanted to give them one final chance to change their minds?"

"You will have to wait and find out tonight with everyone else," smiled Christopher.

Christopher let his arm fall. We joined hands and began walking up along the creek, praying as we went.

"*Father,*" Christopher said softly, "*we ask for you to make your will absolutely clear to us. Speak through the remainder of this day to our hearts and our minds. Place within us the thoughts you want us to have. Direct our thoughts, Lord. Direct them into the channels of your choosing in such a way that we can know they are coming from you and that you mean them to direct the course of our steps. Give me guidance concerning what I am to say this evening. Let my words, whatever is your will concerning the future, speak to the people, even if it be but to one individual, in such a way that life becomes better than it was before—because someone knows you, their Father, in a more personal way.*"

Christopher stopped and sighed. It was a good, contented sigh.

I could tell he felt confident that the decision was in God's hands and that we would be shown what to do.

"*Lord,*" I said, "*give us both the same direction. Confirm to us separately whether this offer is truly from your hand. Guide our steps, guide our thoughts, guide our conversations and prayers as we reflect upon it. We give this decision over into your hands completely.*"

"*Yes, Lord,*" Christopher added, "*we place it entirely into your care. We thank you for this opportunity, and we commit it to you, so that your purposes might be accomplished through it.*"

It fell quiet between us. It was a warm afternoon and as we walked, the smells and sounds of the woods and the creek beside us were wonderfully peaceful.

"Would you like to know what I think . . . personally?" I said after we had gone on a little farther in silence.

"Yes . . . yes I would," replied Christopher.

"I think it sounds rather exciting."

CHAPTER 15

THAT EVENING

The church was nearly as full that evening as it had been in the morning. Word had spread throughout the afternoon of what Christopher had told the committee about deferring his decision, so there was a lot of curiosity about what new thing he was going to say. There were those that figured he had decided against taking the position after all and now wanted to explain his reasons.

"I want to express first of all," Christopher began, "how grateful both my wife Corrie and I are for the warmth of your gracious love toward us. I know how beloved Avery Rutledge was to all of you. In the short time since I have been in Miracle Springs I have been closely enough acquainted with him to know why. Corrie and I spent a good deal of time in the Rutledge home, both before our marriage and since, and we considered Avery and his dear wife to be close and special friends.

"It is not easy for a congregation to lose a man such as Avery— the only pastor this growing church has ever known. In light of that, I consider it a rare honor that you have opened yourselves so quickly and hospitably to me in calling me to fill his now-vacant shoes. Corrie, of course, you have all known as long as you have known your former pastor. But until this morning most of you knew very little about me, and I am humbled that your invitation has been so enthusiastic.

"Naturally, as you might well imagine, my prayers in recent days have been energetic and not without a good deal of emotion. I am, as you know, a native Easterner. Up until a year or two ago,

California might as well have been a foreign country as far as I was concerned."

A few chuckles went around the room.

"Then I had the good fortune to meet and fall in love with the young lady who would become my wife, and suddenly California was the most exciting state in the Union!"

More chuckles followed, and embarrassment on my part. It was always more embarrassing for me to hear someone else talking about me, even than to stand up and do the talking myself.

"To be honest," Christopher went on, "when I told Corrie that I intended to come from Virginia here to Miracle Springs, the only thing I had in mind at the time was to ask her father for her hand in marriage—which, I want publicly to thank him for granting," he added, glancing over to where Pa was sitting. Pa nodded with a smile.

"The point is that I did not stop fully to consider what moving here might mean in terms of my own future. My brain was a little too occupied with Corrie at the time to think about anything beyond seeing her again!"

Christopher paused a moment, and his expression became more thoughtful.

"As you know," he went on, "in recent months I have been planning for us to pursue our future once more in the East. But there has been no clear and distinct leading with regard to that future. Now suddenly I find myself faced with an offer that would essentially make me a *Californian* myself.

"All this is by way of saying that, even though I came to Miracle Springs as a stranger to all but one of you, after the prayer and soul-searching of these past few days since your committee's offer to me, I now realize that I consider this more of a home than any place I have been before. Suddenly thoughts of returning to the East—though Corrie and I are booked on a ship due to leave San Francisco later this very week!—now seem remote and unreal. You heard the story of my early years this morning, and you know what a struggle it has been for me to find a place to call home and to find a family with whom I could know I was loved.

"I *have* found such here, in this place . . . with you. I am more grateful than you can know for the open arms that Drum and

Almeda and their family have held out to me. I feel that same love flowing from the rest of you too. That is what I have come to know with a contentment that I believe has come from my heavenly Father—*this* is my home . . . here with you."

As Christopher paused for a breath, I could tell everyone was touched by what he said. I was dabbing my own eyes, and I saw Almeda doing the same, and here and there a quiet amen sounded in thankful affirmation.

"Therefore, with all that as introduction, I want to reaffirm, as I said this morning, that I *am* prepared to accept your invitation to—"

Before he could even finish the sentence, he was interrupted by more amens and applause from everyone.

Christopher laughed.

"Thank you. You are all very kind. However, you didn't let me finish! And the second thing I was going to say is equally as important as the first."

Again he paused while everyone settled down, curious about what he was going to add.

"I said that I was *prepared* to accept your invitation to become the minister of the Miracle Springs Community Church," he said, giving special emphasis to the word. "Yet just as I felt you needed to know more about me and my background before I could accept your invitation, I think it is only fair that you know more about what kind of a pastor I would be as well. In other words, there remains one further proviso to my acceptance, one further opportunity I must give you to speak now or forever hold your peace, as it were."

There was some shifting around as everyone listened, and Christopher could tell the people were uncertain about what he meant.

"Let me try to explain," he said. "I am a firm believer in not making hasty decisions. I fear that much damage is done by rushing to the conclusion that God is leading in some matter, when we are listening instead to our own emotions and desires. Rarely does one err by waiting.

"However . . ." and here Christopher smiled, "in this present case, we do not have a great deal of time, as Corrie and I have all our worldly possession packed away in preparation to leave for San Francisco the day after tomorrow! Therefore, I must make a decision—and quickly. In order to prevent my mistaking God's leading, therefore, I felt it wise, notwithstanding your vote of this morning, to allow you one final opportunity to reconsider your decision.

"In order to give you what additional information is possible that might cause you to see me in a different light, I want this evening to tell you very candidly why you might want to do so. I would utter no word to sway anyone favorably, to woo or impress. I would have not a single one among you say six months or a year from now, 'If only I had known this . . . I would not have voted in favor of the man.' "

Again Christopher paused, this time to draw in a deep breath.

"Therefore," he continued, "this evening I am going to do my best to tell you what sort of pastor I will likely be. I will say it in a word—I will consider it my sacred duty to *challenge* you, not to pamper you, to challenge you with the same precepts by which I challenge myself.

"If you are uncomfortable with what I say, therefore, it would be good to speak up now and withdraw the call before Corrie and I change our plans. I have seen too many churches get into difficulty with pastors because they knew not what manner of man they were inviting into their pulpit.

"Too often the pulpit is seen as a position of prestige rather than a position of servanthood. I do not see it so. I would have you fully aware of any and every grievance you might someday want to bring against me. I would have us bring our differences into the light ahead of time, so that they do not cause division between us later.

"When I pastored before, in Richmond, the precepts I taught fell unwelcome on many ears. I came to be viewed as something of a radical, as holding fanatical spiritual positions. Most of my congregation wanted a brand of Christianity that would enable them to feel good and retain the comforts to which their societal positions entitled them, but which would exact no cost—no cost to their *selves*, no cost to their pride, no cost to their time or bank accounts. They did not *want* to be challenged. Their desire was for a restful Christianity which made few demands upon the conscience. Servanthood and self-sacrifice were in no wise elements of their spiritual creed. My words, therefore, were unwelcome in their ears.

"The situation grew untenable, and when I finally left that pastorate my vision for the ministry was at death's door. I vowed I would never again seek a pulpit, nor would I ever occupy one without ascertaining first whether the congregation desired the brand of Christianity which burns in my heart. Knowing our late friend Avery Rutledge as I feel I did, I think I know the answer to my question already. After hearing him preach only a time or two, I knew I had discovered a kindred spirit. However, I must be faithful to this commitment I made to myself several years ago.

"This is why I say I am prepared to accept your invitation. I said so this morning, and I say so again. But I want again to give *you* the final say in the matter of a decision. For with me in this pulpit, you *will* be challenged, even as I challenge myself. You *will* be confronted with servanthood and self-denial, even as I attempt to live out those truths in my own life. You *will* be called upon to examine the cost of following Jesus and of heeding the voice of your conscience. What we will seek together will not be cozy, comfortable Christianity, but rather the discipleship of sacrificial Christlikeness.

"If I am your pastor, I will see it as my duty and obligation, as I said, to challenge, not to pamper. I will not hope to send you back to your homes every Sunday not feeling warm and comfortable, but rather with the same prayerful discomforts with which I am myself afflicted.

"Is this what you want? Then I am your man. Is this *not* what you want? Then I am *not* your man.

"Do these bold words strike fear in your hearts? Perhaps you find the spirit of indignation rising up within you, whispering into your ear, *Who does the presumptuous young fellow think he is?*"

Christopher paused and looked throughout the silent church.

"I would have you examine your reactions," he added, "be they favorable *or* negative. I would have you be anything but lukewarm and noncommittal, because nothing is more killing to a growing faith than that."

Again he paused, this time with a very serious expression.

"I leave the matter before you one final time," he said, "—Corrie, if you would join me . . ." Christopher said, stepping down and walking to where I sat. He offered his arm. I stood and took it. "Drum, Almeda, and the rest of you," Christopher added, looking at Zack, Tad, Becky, and Ruth, "I think it might be best for all of you to come with us as well, so that the church can be free to discuss the matter."

He now turned and addressed the congregation again.

"We will leave you now and return home. I encourage you to discuss the matter openly and with forthrightness. Anyone with objections, please voice them now, for the good of the church. Patrick," he said, nodding toward Mr. Shaw, "—I turn the rest of the service over to you. Goodnight and God bless you all."

Christopher and I walked down the aisle and outside the somber church, followed by the rest of the family.

CHAPTER 16

MOVING BACK IN

Mr. Shaw, Mr. Harding, and Agnes Bosely came to the house again the following morning about eleven o'clock. Katie was already there, so we had been expecting them.

"You're still our man, Christopher!" said Patrick Shaw as Christopher and I walked out to greet their buggy.

"Katie tells us there was a lively discussion," replied Christopher.

"You stirred things up just a bit by what you said."

"Good!" laughed Christopher. "I was hoping to. A complacent church is a stagnant church."

"After your message yesterday morning everyone was favorable and sympathetic," laughed Mr. Harding. "Then last night you gave them more to think about than many expected."

"Sometimes a good shaking is just what the doctor ordered," rejoined Christopher.

"Well, the long and the short of it," now put in Mr. Shaw, "is that nothing has changed. Both the church and we as the committee want you as our next pastor."

"Thank you, Patrick," replied Christopher. "Was the vote unanimous this time?"

Mr. Shaw glanced over at the other three a little nervously.

"Actually . . . no, it wasn't," replied Mr. Harding.

"But tell him, too, Douglas, that there were only three dissenting votes," added Aunt Katie hastily.

All eyes now turned toward Christopher, waiting to see how he would respond.

"I'm glad to hear it!" he said. "After the things I said last evening, if you had said it was unanimous, I would either not have believed you or else would have known that *somebody* wasn't speaking up. There are *always* objections to Christianity that challenges people. Knowing that some objections *were* aired sets my mind at ease that probably most of the negative reactions had a chance to be voiced. If, after that, the vote was still so close to unanimous, then I am very encouraged."

"You are not put off by the fact that three individuals voted against you?"

Christopher laughed. "Certainly not. That will keep things interesting!"

"Do you want to know who the three were?"

"I have no interest in knowing. Although," he laughed, "I'm sure I shall find out soon enough. The objectors in any church usually manage to make their voices heard more determinedly than the rest."

"Well then. . . ?" said Mrs. Bosely.

"Then . . . what?" rejoined Christopher.

"What is your answer?"

"About the invitation?"

The heads of all four of the committee members nodded up and down in unison.

"I would say that if Corrie and I are going to stay here in Miracle Springs . . . then we have some unpacking to do!"

I shrieked with delight and threw my arms around him.

We were staying!

"And I'd better go straight into town," Christopher added, "and telegraph San Francisco to see about a refund on our tickets!"

CHAPTER 17

PARTINGS

Two days later, as if to temper the exuberance I felt at our not leaving Miracle Springs, the federal marshal came to pay a visit to Zack.

"I'm afraid I've got to take your prisoner, son," he said.

"Where?" asked Zack.

"Down to Sacramento. He's going to have to stand trial down there. I know it's personal for you, and I understand how you feel, but it can't be helped."

Zack nodded. "How . . . how, uh—bad is it, Marshal?"

"Well, there ain't no murder warrants on him, if that's what you mean—"

Zack breathed a sigh of relief at the marshal's words.

"—so he ain't likely to hang. Leastways there ain't nothing been found yet. But there's plenty else, from a long while back, up north in the state and in the Nevada territory. We're still waiting to hear from the East."

"How much jail time you figure he'll face?"

"No way to tell, son. No way at all."

After Zack told us about it at supper that same evening, all the happiness that had been around the place for the past two days seemed to evaporate all at once.

It was real silent around the table. We'd known this day was coming, and as fond as we'd grown of Jesse Harris, we knew he still had to pay for what he'd done in his past. It was one of those hard and sad things in life where there just didn't seem to be any resolution to a situation other than a painful one.

"When's he have to go, son?" asked Pa.

"Marshal's taking him tomorrow."

"What time?"

"Middle of the morning, I reckon. There's some paper work we gotta take care of."

"Good," Pa nodded, "that'll give us all time to go into town and say goodbye to Jesse."

I knew every one of us around the table were thinking the same thing—that it might really be a *goodbye*.

Again it was silent.

"Well . . . God bless him," said Christopher. "He's God's son now, and his future's in God's hands."

The next day came. Like Pa'd said, we all went into town to see Jesse Harris off. Our whole family crowded into his jail cell. Zack had to stay outside after locking us in, but he joined in with the rest of us through the bars. We prayed with Mr. Harris one last time. We were all in there praying when the marshal walked into Zack's office, and he could hardly believe what he was seeing.

"I'm sure sorry you have to go away, Mr. Harris," said Tad.

Mr. Harris looked him straight in the eye. "Not half as sorry as I am about how I spent my life, son," he replied seriously. "Even though I feel like a different man, I ain't chafin' about having to make restitution for what I done. I know the good Lord's forgiven me, but the law still says I gotta pay."

Then the marshal and Zack got Mr. Harris all ready to go, and of course they had to tie him up and everything. Then he and the marshal walked to the station.

All the rest of us followed along so that you would have thought some kind of local hero was leaving town rather than an outlaw. The marshal kept shaking his head and muttering that it was the strangest kind of thing he'd ever seen in his life. Mr. Harris promised to explain it to him on the train ride down to Sacramento. From what Zack had said about his conversations with the man Unger, I had no doubt it would be a very interesting talk.

They boarded the train, and we all waved goodbye as it pulled out, just like I'd imagined it would be with me and Christopher.

Yet there we were standing on the platform with everyone else, waving to Mr. Harris instead.

Christopher and I walked slowly back into town hand in hand.

"Well, he's completely the Lord's now," said Christopher after some time. "Now I feel able to look to the future—even more than last weekend when the church voted."

"How do you mean?" I asked.

"Oh, I don't know exactly . . . almost like the continued uncertainty about Jesse's future kept a certain doubt or anxiety in the air. Maybe it's only that I knew it was weighing on Zack."

"You really think it was?"

Christopher nodded. "He didn't say much about it, but I know he was concerned. I'm sure he probably still is, but at least any decision about it is out of his hands. Maybe now that he can get on with his future, I can get on with mine too."

"Are you excited?" I asked.

"Oh yes! Just imagine, Corrie—I'm a pastor again! Can you believe it?"

"Of course I can," I laughed. "What are you going to do?"

"You mean. . . ?"

"I mean first . . . right now. What's the *first* thing you are going to do as pastor of Miracle Springs?"

Christopher thought a moment or two.

"Well, we were so busy yesterday unpacking and celebrating and talking," he said, "—now that you bring it up, I realize that there's one important *first* thing we've neglected to do as we make this new beginning in our lives."

"What?" I asked.

"Come with me. I want you to do it with me."

CHAPTER 18

A NEW BEGINNING

Christopher led me straight to the church on the other side of town.

We didn't talk anymore as we walked along, first down the street that led through the middle of town and then along past several rows of houses. We walked slowly, still holding hands, nodding to whoever we met. But Christopher was subdued, and I knew he was praying for the town and its people. So was I.

After leaving the main part of town and walking across an open field, we reached the church. We stopped fifty or so feet from it. Christopher gazed up at the simple white building and steeple, seeing it, I think, with different eyes than before. This was *his* church now, something he had never anticipated. And the reason for it was still a fresh pain for us both, because Rev. Rutledge had only been dead a week.

I suppose it was *my* church now too!

Goodness—I was a *minister's wife* . . . something I had never anticipated either! If only Ma could see me now—married and wife of a pastor.

My husband even said I was pretty—that was something *Ma* never anticipated!

I smiled at the memory. *Well*, I thought, *I guess she can see me. I sure wish I knew what she thinks!*

Christopher started walking again and led me the rest of the way up the steps and inside.

It was a warm day, yet the chill from the previous night still lingered inside the building. It was quiet and still, such a different feeling than when everyone was present on Sunday. I suppose it was like any other quiet empty building, yet there was something different about it too. It felt reverent and holy, like God really was there. I know he is everywhere all the time, and no more in a church than in a barn or someone's house or out in the open country. Of course, he's in people's hearts most of all. Yet still, there was a special kind of sense of his presence in this little church building as we walked inside.

The Miracle Springs church contained so many memories for me—Pa and Rev. Rutledge helping to build it, Uncle Nick and Pa's weddings (and mine!), and so many wonderful times through the years. I almost felt as if I could hear faint echoes of Avery Rutledge's voice. Little snatches of sermons he had preached through the years came back to me—so much that had helped me grow and mature as a Christian. I thought of him and Harriet and how as a couple too they had helped me, of how many times I had been in their home, talking and praying with them, asking them questions.

There truly was something wonderfully full when a man and woman ministered together as the Rutledges had. And now suddenly it dawned on me—Christopher and I would be in that position in this community from now on. We would be the Rutledges!

People would look to *us* for help and counsel. Maybe even young women would come to talk to *me*, as I had the Rutledges, asking me their questions about life and God and growing up and what God might want for their lives.

The thought was overwhelming at first. In many ways I still felt so young. When I stopped to think about it, I didn't really feel so much different than I had at fifteen, or twenty-one, or twenty-seven. Yet I was different. I suppose in the eyes of those much younger than myself, like little Ruth, I was a grown woman. I had always thought of myself as just a girl. Being married had changed that perception quite a bit in my own eyes, but this would, in some ways, be an even greater change. Now the whole community would be looking up to Christopher and me. Even if we didn't necessarily feel worthy of it, how could they help it?

Christopher Braxton was the *pastor* of Miracle Springs, and Corrie Hollister Braxton was his wife!

We sat down in the front row of seats, and then, as if he had been reading my mind, Christopher spoke.

"It is really a humbling thing," he said, "when people place so much trust in you that they say they want you to be their spiritual leader."

I nodded. I knew exactly what he was feeling.

"I am excited about the prospects for the future, yet . . . there is always that frightening aspect of it too—what if you let people down?"

"You won't," I said.

"I did in the only other church I pastored."

"That was different."

"Perhaps, but I still can't help the worry of it crossing my mind."

We were both quiet several minutes as we sat in the stillness thinking about the change that was coming to our lives.

"I wanted to come here to pray," said Christopher at length. "Will you pray with me?"

"Of course."

"I always said to myself that if the Lord ever blessed me with the opportunity to minister in this way again, the first thing I would do would be to commit that ministry, the church, and all the people involved to him in prayer. I forgot about it yesterday, and then just this morning remembered."

"You've been praying all along," I said.

"Yes, but I mean placing it specifically into his hands—saying that all this ministry is *his*, not mine."

"I see," I said.

Again we were quiet, and then we closed our eyes. Again, Christopher took my hand.

"*Oh, God our Father,*" he prayed softly after about a minute, "*we are both so deeply thankful for this opportunity you have given us. We grieve at the loss of our dear brother Avery and for his dear family. Yet we know he is with you—happy, smiling, radiant, and full of life. May we be worthy and able to carry on the work he began and performed so faithfully.*"

Christopher paused and breathed in deeply.

"*We are humbled, yet excited,*" he prayed again. "*And we pray that you would keep us humble, and keep us excited. Let us be enthusiastic about your work among your people, and never think that it is our work, or that lives are changed by our efforts. But we do ask you, dear Father, to change lives—not by our efforts or through our ministry, but by your Spirit which is alive and at work wherever men and women live. And if it pleases you to involve us in that life-changing process, then even more deeply will we rejoice at your goodness to us. We do thank you, Lord, that we are yours, and that you have changed our lives. We want nothing so much in all the world as to proclaim that good news throughout the land that you love your children, that you are a good Father to them, and that they may trust you. Oh, Father, make those truths known to the sons and daughters of your making!"*

I squeezed Christopher's hand as he paused again. My heart was full of the same prayer, though I could find no words to say beyond what he had already prayed.

"And now, Lord," he continued, *"we do give ourselves and the future of our ministry here into your hands. We commit this church, its people, its families, all those who will come here in future years, and especially ourselves—we commit all to you. We ask, Father, that you accomplish your purposes for this church and its people. May we bring nothing of our own to bear upon what we do here, but only what you would have us do."*

Christopher stopped again, and now I prayed.

"We ask for you to specially touch every single person, whether man or woman or boy or girl," I said, *"who comes into this church. Touch them, Lord, not by what Christopher or I may say or do, but because you are here."*

"And may your Spirit be here always, God," said Christopher. *"May people feel your presence just by being here."*

"And I pray, too, Lord, for our home," I said. *"May our home, wherever it is, whether our bunkhouse or somewhere else someday— may our home be what the Rutledges has always been for me—a place of warmth and welcome and open-hearted hospitality. Bring people to us, Lord, that we can help in some way. Let where we live be like the church itself, and I ask that the community will know that Christopher and I love each one of them and that they can come to us any time."*

"You don't know how much it means to me to hear you say that," said Christopher, and it took me a moment to realize that he was speaking to me, no longer praying. "Something about this feels so different than before, back in Richmond. As I said, you just can't imagine how it warms my heart to know that you want to share this ministry with me, that you care about the same things I do, that you want to be involved in people's lives in the same way I do."

"Isn't that what being married is all about?" I said.

Christopher smiled. "I suppose," he replied, "but that makes me no less thankful for you."

CHAPTER 19

A VISION FOR MINISTRY

"What are you going to *do*, Christopher," I asked as we continued to sit together in the church, "—next, this week, next week? What does a pastor do besides lead the service on Sunday? I've never been married to a pastor before—"

"I should hope not!"

"You know what I mean. This is all new to me. I haven't been to seminary. I don't know what you did in Richmond."

"Are you asking, not so much what am I going to do, but what are *we* going to do?"

"Maybe I am," I answered.

"Well, set your mind at ease—you don't have to do anything. What I mean is that I don't expect anything of you besides what you normally do. Just be yourself and go on with life as always."

"You mean stay at home, work in the freight company?"

"Exactly. Believe me, you'll be plenty involved in due time. Women will come to you, just like they did to Harriet, wanting to talk. You'll call on people with me."

"I can't help being a little nervous," I said.

"That's understandable. But it will all come about very naturally."

"What will *you* do, then?"

"My, but you are persistent with that question!"

I laughed. "I'm just interested."

"I know," replied Christopher, then paused to think.

"Believe it or not," he said, "I have been considering that very

99

thing ever since leaving the church in Richmond. I've often said to myself, 'What will I do the next time, if the Lord ever gives me another church? How would I begin a new ministry?' Now here I am with a chance to put into practice what I've concluded."

"What is that?"

"Well," Christopher began, "it has seemed to me, as I have reflected on it, that one of the great hindrances to effective ministry is that people tend to see a pastor as *different* from other people, as a man whose profession it is to be more spiritual than the rest. In a sense, they view their pastor or priest as the person responsible for taking care of the spiritual side of life so they don't have to do much about it themselves. It may seem a harsh thing to say, but I think that's why many people give money to support the church— almost as a way of paying someone *else* to be spiritual on their behalf. It's just the age-old problem of indulgences dressed up to look like faithful tithing."

"I've never heard you talk about this kind of thing before."

Christopher smiled. "I don't suppose I ever saw the need. I told you way back when we were together in Virginia that the ministry was a part of the past that I had put behind me until the Lord did something to change that fact. When a few months ago he did cause me to start thinking about it again, I kept quiet at first because—well, you know, because I thought it meant we were supposed to go back to the East. But along with that, I found myself thinking about all these things again. There just never came a time I felt was right to tell you about it."

"So how are you going to keep people from looking at you as different?"

"The first and most important thing is to show people that the pastor is *not* different from the rest of them," replied Christopher. "That's how I want people to see Christopher Braxton—not first as a pastor who walks and talks and acts different than the rest, who wears a clerical aura, so to speak, but just as a member of the community. A man's not a minister because he's a professional Christian, but because he feels he has something to contribute to the quality of life in a community—daily life, everyone's life, the kind of spirituality that is supposed to be intrinsic to *everyone's* existence. I don't think a minister can do that unless people view him as one of them. You have to keep that wall of separation from going up between the people sitting down here and the man standing up there."

Christopher pointed up to the pulpit, where he had spoken to the congregation just a few days ago.

"I realize, of course," he went on, "that one of the important aspects of a minister's role is to teach people things about life with God that they aren't aware of. But that teaching and preaching has got to be just one part of that role, and it has to emerge out of a life that is shared with the people of the community at very basic levels. In other words, I hope that people will see as much of you and me in their homes and in our home and in town and at the freight company and in their fields and barns and kitchens as they will in this church. So often the only time people see a minister is standing in front of the church on Sunday morning or in town and still all dressed up in his best clothes. If that's the only way they see him, what else can it lead to but the professional clerical image—he's someone who is paid to be spiritual, as I said before, when they have to work hard from day to day just to put food on the table. Why, I may stand up there some Sundays in my work trousers and shirt just to remind people of that sameness."

I laughed. "You don't really mean it?"

"I do mean it. And why not?"

"So we're going to visit people a lot, I take it?" I said.

"Yes we are. And not as the pastor and his wife, but as their friends, as a man and woman who care about them."

"I'm glad. I don't know about you wearing your work clothes on Sunday, but I do like the visiting part of it."

"That's one of the first things I determined I would do if I ever pastored again, and I can't wait to get started—I'm going to personally call on every single person in this town, the saloon girls and Franklin Royce the banker and all the rest. Everyone. And not with a lot of spiritual talk either—just to shake their hand and tell them you and I are around if ever we can help them."

"That will raise some eyebrows," I laughed, "and set tongues wagging—if Mrs. Sinclair sees you walking into the Gold Nugget! Or Mr. Royce's bank, for that matter, after all he's done to people over the years."

"Let them say what they will."

"Do you really think a saloon girl or a banker would come to you or me for help?" I asked.

"I don't know—but we've got to be the ones to make the first move, to extend our hands. Maybe we have to make the first several moves. A minister can't sit alone in the church day after day studying his Bible and writing out sermons, waiting for people to come to him, he's got to be out and part of the community every day. That's how people learn to trust him, and eventually to pay attention when he says, 'God is our Father, yours and mine, and we can trust him more than we've been in the habit of doing.' I don't intend to write out any sermons, in fact. I'm just going to talk to people about God and tell them what kind of Father he is and how they can go about living for him and pleasing him."

"But even calling on people doesn't necessarily make them see you differently," I said. "Remember how awkward it has been between you and Tom Woodstock since we began visiting them."

"I know. It takes time. But after I helped him with his fence a time or two, at least he began to talk a little. And you and Jennie have had some good talks, which I don't think would have happened had we not been persistent to involve ourselves in their lives."

"But you can't go work with *every* man in the community like you did with Tom and his fence."

"Why not?"

"Because you're the pastor now. You'll have church things to do."

"What could be more the business of the church than that?"

CHAPTER 20

FAMILY TITHES

The following Sunday, feeling almost like newcomers to Miracle Springs all over again, Christopher and I walked into church. I was so happy, and everyone greeted us so warmly.

We were to have been on a ship steaming south along the coast of Mexico by now. Yet here we were back in the Miracle Springs church. Then it dawned on me yet again—I was the pastor's wife!

The singing was so enthusiastic, and all the announcements and prayers even seemed to be more energetic than usual. When Christopher finally began to talk, everyone was full of anticipation of what he might say after all his warnings of the previous week.

"This morning I would like to do my best to tell you what I believe," he said. "You may call this a sermon or a testimonial of faith or whatever you like. Whatever you call it, I want to outline as concisely as I am able the spiritual principles by which I try to order my life. While I am your pastor, it will be these principles that I will teach and emphasize and that I will constantly hearken back to. These principles are the foundation of my life, my ministry, my views. They were the cornerstones of my prior years of church ministry and will be the building blocks of however long a ministry the Lord sees fit for me to have among you. Presumably you will either grow with me according to these priorities I will outline, or else one day you will decide to terminate my pastorate.

"Let me say very clearly that these are the principles by which I *try* to order my life. I cannot say that I *do* live perfectly by them, or do even a tolerable job of it. These represent my *goals* in life,

103

what I aim and strive and pray for, *not* what I think I presently am capable of. This life is an attempt, a journey we all share—pastor and congregation alike. It is a journey we must embark on *because of* our imperfection, not because I, or anyone, think he or she really lives these principles as they ought to be lived.

"Yet with God's help, we *shall* become capable of living them. It is my conviction that he wants us not merely to dream about these truths, but to have them become reality in our lives."

Christopher stopped and glanced about, then a slow smile spread over his face.

"Before I begin with the deeper aspects of what I want to share with you this morning, let us take care of a very practical matter that all churches have to deal with and that everyone wonders about from time to time. Let's talk about money, for obviously, if I am going to be your pastor, Corrie and I must have money to live."

He paused again. A little squirming about went on in the seats, and I must admit that I felt an embarrassed twinge starting to creep up the back of my neck. Money could be such an awkward subject, and I didn't think I could bear it if Christopher started off the first Sunday by asking people to give us money.

"Before we continue, would a couple of you men come forward and pass around these two collection plates here."

Pa glanced around, then rose. Mr. Douglas joined him, and they came forward and stood in front of Christopher.

"I want to urge you all to examine your hearts," said Christopher. "If you feel the Lord has been gracious to you, then repay to him accordingly and give generously. Let us pray. *Lord, give us thankful hearts for your goodness to us, and may we each return abundantly to you from your provision to us. Amen.*"

Pa and Mr. Douglas now went through the church with the plates while Harriet played a hymn on the piano. I still felt awkward and kept my eyes looking down in my lap. I heard occasional shuffling about, and now and then the tinkling sound of coins being dropped into the plate.

In a minute or two the men took the plates back up to Christopher and resumed their seats.

Christopher took them and glanced at the contents of both.

"Good," he said with a big smile, "very nice indeed! It would appear you have been most generous." Then he jiggled the plates about in his two hands a little, so that you could hear the money bouncing around.

Christopher, I thought, *what are you doing?* I was getting seriously embarrassed.

"Now, let me ask you a question," he said, still holding the plates. "What is this money for? Who did you give it to?"

The church was completely silent.

"Come on," Christopher insisted. "Who is this for?"

"We give it to you and yer missus, preacher!" someone called out from the back.

Christopher gazed back at the congregation.

"Is that what the rest of you think as well?" he asked. A few nods gradually went around, along with some low murmurings of assent.

"I see. All right, then, now I want to do something with this money which may come as a surprise."

Christopher stepped forward and handed one of the plates back to Harriet, who was sitting in the front row on the right side, and the other to me, in the front row of the left.

"I want to pass these plates back among you," he said. "If any of you right now finds yourself in such financial straits that you scarcely know where your next meal is coming from, I want you to take from the plate when it comes to you. Take whatever you feel will meet your need until next week."

Slowly Harriet and I looked at Christopher, then passed our plates to those seated next to us. Everyone was quiet. No one knew quite what to think.

"I am absolutely serious," Christopher went on. "The rest of you keep your eyes down. No one need see what his neighbor is doing. This is no cause for embarrassment. If you have need, then in God's name I urge you to receive this provision from his hand through your fellow church members."

It was so silent you could have heard a pin drop as the plates now went through the church again, with now and then the slightest tinkling sound, though I couldn't tell if anyone was doing as Christopher had said or if the sound was just from the plates being passed. A few minutes later they made their way back up to the front, and Christopher took them again from Harriet and me, then set them down on the table in front of the pulpit.

"I know this proceeding may seem a bit unusual, but I did it to make a point," said Christopher. "This will be the nature of the tithes and offerings we bring to the Lord in the future. As you know, when the tithe was introduced in the Old Testament, it was usually given in the form of grain rather than money. This grain was stored in what the Bible calls storehouses, for use either in times of famine or to feed the poor. Now while it is true that the priests of Israel received their sustenance from these tithes, they were not primarily given in order to pay the priests. They were given to provide for the people themselves. And such shall be our tithes here while I am your pastor.

"You all know the deep and abiding respect I had for Avery Rutledge. My plan has no bearing whatever on his ministry nor the honor in which I hold him. But I am a young man. I have hoisted great sacks of grain on my back and worked Drum Hollister's mine with what I hope was sufficient strength to earn his favor.

"Therefore, as I told you last week, I will take no salary as your pastor. Not so much as a penny from these plates will be used by Corrie and me. I will work with my hands and my back and my legs for our bread, as the rest of you do, and I will pastor your church as one of its laborers, not as one who is paid to speak to you on Sundays.

"The money we collect from Sunday to Sunday will be in the way of *family tithes*, which we will place in our friend Franklin Royce's 'storehouse' to be used, as was the grain of the Israelites of old, in times of famine and to feed our poor. We will each give to the Lord out of the abundance of his provision to us, and we will use the contents of our tithe-granaries for those of our community in need, when crops fail, when fire comes, when death visits unexpectedly. When you give, therefore, you will be giving to your neighbors. It may even be your own family that will one day find itself in need."

Christopher paused, and again smiled so as to lighten the atmosphere.

Everyone stared at him from their seats. They had never heard anything like this before. And although Christopher and I had already discussed what he was proposing, I was still amazed by how much sense it made. I thought I had known most of what there was to know about Christopher, and yet I continued to be surprised by—and sometimes even in awe of—this man I had married.

"You can see, therefore," Christopher said, "that I am going to need work from Sunday to Sunday. I am capable of most things and am an eager learner. As I said earlier, Corrie and I are going to need money to live. But I would ask you to give me opportunity to labor for that provision. I have worked for many of you already and I am willing to do anything—from cleaning stalls to stringing fence wire to digging ditches—and I know a fair amount about construction and livestock. I will not be able to work a full ten or twelve hours every day, for there will be times, of course, when I will need to carry out my pastoral function during the daytime hours. But I should think myself able to give forty or forty-five hours in honest labor most weeks and will appreciate any opportunities you can give me to serve you in this way.

"Now, Harriet," he said, glancing over to where she sat, "perhaps we could have a hymn before I begin my sermon."

CHAPTER 21

WHO IS GOD?

The pause which followed the singing was lengthy. Christopher closed his eyes for a moment. I knew he was breathing a last-minute prayer, asking God to do his will and accomplish his purposes through the words Christopher was about to say.

When he opened his eyes and drew in a deep breath, there was such purpose, such a keen look of intensity and vision on his face, that my heart swelled up in pride and gratitude to God all over again for the man he had given me to share life with.

I thought again as Christopher spoke, about the first days and weeks of our meeting at Mrs. Timms' farm. Even though he was the same person now, there had been such a discouragement evident then, even a sense of failure which now I understood more fully. He honestly hadn't known whether he would ever be in a position to speak to people through a church again.

Yet here he was, standing before the people of Miracle Springs, brave to say what he believed without apology, with such light in his wonderful eyes and such strength in his voice.

I was so happy for him, happy that the Lord was giving him the desire of his heart in this new place, in a new way, with new friends. I was happy that he was my husband and that the Lord had blessed me to be able to share this ministry with him. And I was very happy we weren't on that ship bound for New York!

"Over the next weeks, as I said," Christopher began, "I would like to tell you what I believe. I would like to share the principles that will form the cornerstones of my ministry among you because they form the cornerstones of my life. These are not principles I learned at the Bible Institute or from some book or from a sermon I once heard, but truths I have come to discover as central to the Christian faith in my years of walking with God. Some of them have come from my first pastorate in Richmond. Others came during my years alone as foreman of a farm. Some emerged out of long lonely walks when my heart and mind were full of questions. What I am saying is that these truths have come to me slowly, over many years.

"They comprise three chief areas. The first has to do with the character and nature of God himself—who God actually *is*.

"We say we worship and seek to obey God. But do we know what kind of God he is? Do we know what he is *like*, if I may say it . . . as a person? Too often, I fear, we do not. I certainly did not in my younger years. I have had to learn and discover who God is. This is why I believe knowing what God is like is such an important aspect of what it means to be a Christian. This is what I will talk about with you this morning."

Suddenly a little voice from somewhere in the congregation sounded.

"God's like my daddy!" it said.

The high-pitched comment from the five- or six-year-old girl was so unexpected that Christopher burst into laughter, followed by all the rest of us.

"Sally, you are exactly right!" Christopher said. "You've been paying attention better than anyone! I'm going to talk about that very thing this morning."

Christopher waited for the laughter to gradually die down, his along with everyone else's. Then he returned to his sermon.

"The second area," he said, "which I will discuss next week, is this: What is the nature of faith? Once we know who God is, what does it mean to believe in him, to have faith in him?

"And the third area will concern itself with the question, What is God's purpose in our lives? When we know God and have faith in him, then what does God want to accomplish with us? What is the work he wants to do within your heart and mine?

"When I say the words, *I, Christopher Braxton, am a Christian*, what I mean is based upon my answers to these three questions:

Who is God? What is faith? What is God's purpose in my life? I hope our discussion of them will help you clarify what *you* mean when you say that you are a Christian."

Christopher paused and took a breath.

"All right," he said with a smile, "any questions so far?"

He paused and waited.

"Sally's shown she's not afraid to speak up. How about the rest of you?"

But no one said anything. The congregation just took the opportunity to shuffle themselves about again in their seats.

"Well then, let's begin, shall we?" Christopher went on. "This morning let us look at the first of these three questions: *Who is God?*

"I said at the beginning that I want to try to explain to you what I believe. At the very core of my faith, I believe that the central truth in all the universe is simply this: *God is our good and loving Father.*

"Now, we know that God is love. We have been taught and have heard those words all our lives. But what else is he?

"He is our Father.

"If there is one thing I will undoubtedly speak to you over and over about it is this one foundational fact of existence—God's Fatherhood.

"So I would answer the question, *Who is God?* by saying that he is our eternal heavenly Father, our loving Creator.

"Discovering this personal loving Fatherhood within each of our own hearts is the mountaintop of Christianity. There is nothing else the Christian faith is about. By his own admission, this was the reason Jesus came, the reason he taught, the reason he shed his blood—to show us what the Father is like and how to live as sons and daughters of the Father and how to enter into his presence. Jesus came to take our hands and lead us on an upward quest into the high mountains of faith where Fatherhood dwells.

"You see, *God is love* can remain a little abstract for us, mainly because the words are so familiar. Even the word *God* is a high and abstract word. But *father* . . . there is a down-to-earth word that is anything but abstract.

"Now, as I explained to you last week, coming into this realization that God is a good and loving Father was extremely difficult for me. These things I say about God's goodness are no mere platitudes, but truths I have had to fight and struggle to make my own. That is why I now believe them with such passion. For the majority of my life, as I told you, the word *father* conveyed anything *but* goodness. I equated the word with *tyrant*.

"Now I know otherwise. Now I know that it is the tenderest and most loving word in all the world. And this is exactly what we must discover about Fatherhood, whatever has been our response to the word *father* in the past.

"God is not merely our Father in the abstract, as I said, but in very practical and personal ways. We are to be his children. We are to look up to him and call him *Father*—the most intimate and personal and warm address that the human tongue can whisper.

"Do you want to know this Father who is more father to you than you yet have any idea? Do you want to learn how to look up and call him *Father*?

"It takes spending time with him. Call it prayer, call it dialogue—I wish you all could have heard old Alkali Jones talk to God, simply, just like he talked to any of us. Call this sort of conversation anything you wish. I call it just this—talking to him, developing my relationship with my Father just like a growing child does with his parents, talking things over, telling him my struggles and frustrations, sharing with him my doubts and confusions. Who better to tell than my Father? As I told you last week, just learning to say the word was difficult for me at first. It is no different than a child learning to say *mama* or *papa*. It takes practice. We must *learn* to address God in this father-child intimacy."

Christopher paused, then a smile spread over his face.

"Sally," he said, "would you come up here please?"

The dark-headed little girl who had spoken earlier was obviously surprised to hear her name called in the middle of the sermon. Her boldness turned to bashfulness, and now she tried to melt into her seat. Her mother leaned over and whispered to her, urging her to go on up and stand by Christopher. Slowly she stood and walked forward. When she got up beside Christopher, she turned around, saw the congregation, and giggled. Everybody else started to laugh a little too.

Christopher got down on one knee beside the little girl and put his arm around her.

"Sally," he said, "where's your daddy?"

She looked at him with a puzzled expression.

"Where is he, Sally?" he repeated.

"You can see him," she said finally, "—he's right there!" She pointed as she spoke, then started to laugh.

The whole church was enjoying this!

"Bill," said Christopher, glancing in the direction of Sally's finger, "would you come up here and get your daughter?"

The bearded young man looked over at his wife, then smiled, stood, and walked forward. He reached out his arms, and little Sally ran forward and grabbed on to him. Her father clutched her and picked her up in his arms.

"Folks," said Christopher, motioning toward them, "this young girl now feels safe in her father's embrace. And this is exactly the Father-child intimacy I am speaking of when I say *this* is what God desires with each one of us.

"Thank you, Bill—and thank you too, Sally," he added. "You may sit down again."

As they returned to their seats, most eyes followed them, and not many missed the smile on Sally's face as she climbed into her daddy's lap.

Christopher took a couple of breaths and waited a few seconds to allow the mood to grow thoughtful once more.

"If I am to know the Father," he went on at length, "I need to spend just as much time *listening* to him as I do talking to him. That's how to get to know him. That's how we acquaint ourselves with what kind of Father he is . . . by listening to hear his still small voice as it speaks to our minds and hearts.

"Teaching you how to call him Father, as I myself will all my life long be learning more and more intimately to call him Father, taking hands, you and me, as we make this pilgrimage together up the mountain—such will be the purpose of my ministry among you. If you have no interest in becoming sons and daughters to a God who wants us to call him Father, then I fear we will not be able to do much spiritual business together. Because to this and no other purpose is my life dedicated.

"Now along with the fact that God is our Father, I believe that there are certain attributes which define his character. The foundational of these are love, goodness, and trustworthiness. None of these will sound new or radical in your ears. I am sure you are all very familiar with these words.

"However, we do not customarily go very far in truly believing these things about God. Most of us, if we admit it, are *afraid* of God, afraid of his punishment, afraid of his anger. Furthermore, we don't trust him when things go wrong in our lives, and we question his goodness when difficulties arise.

"Why? Because we have not deeply considered what it means that the Father is, in fact, *completely* loving, *completely* good, and *completely* trustworthy.

"This, then, will be another aspect toward which I will attempt continually to point—that there are no circumstances in which God is not fully *loving*, fully *good*, and fully *to be trusted*.

"It may sound at the outset as though this will not be so taxing a truth upon the intellect. But believe me, before we are through considering the implications of the words I have just spoken, you will find many of your previous notions about God shaken to their very depths.

"When your crops fail, when the gold in your mine runs out, when your cattle all take sick and mysteriously die, when illness comes to your family and children, when a loved one is taken from you in death, when your wife dies in childbirth . . . what will you *then* look for from your minister? If at such times you want only dour-faced condolences, then do not look to this pulpit for them.

"I will sympathize in your grief. I will pray with you. I will offer what comfort I am able. I offered myself earlier as a man willing to be employed as a laborer in your community to put bread on my table. I will go ever further. If you cannot afford to hire my time but have work for me to do, I beg you to give me the opportunity to work for and beside you with my own hands without pay in order to put bread on *your* table. Truly I will seek to be your servant. But through all adversity, no matter how severe, I will always remind you that God's goodness reigns supreme. After praying with you in your loss, therefore, I will make you look up into the face of your Father, and say to him, *'Thank you, Father, that you are good . . . that you love me . . . and that I may trust you!'*

"The natural human tendency is just the opposite. The first one upon whom we usually vent the anger of our weakness is God himself. He to whom we should immediately run in the midst of our trouble is the one we instead blame for our circumstances.

"What small-minded creatures we are. *Curse God and die* is the cry of unbelief in the midst of adversity. Yet there may come times when you will want to curse me, your pastor, for continually saying, 'God is good and we may trust him in *all* things.' We would often rather wallow in our sorrows than stand up, cast our eyes toward heaven, and thank him for being a good, loving, and trustworthy Father.

"It is not easy to believe such truths in the anguish of bitter heartache and disappointment. But believe them we *must* if we are to grow into intimacy with him. Believe them we *must* if we are to become his mature sons and daughters.

"I said last week that I did not subscribe to the theory of let the buyer beware. Perhaps I should emphasize that I *do* believe, in our present circumstances, in the theory of let the *congregation* beware! Perhaps my former parishioners were correct in labeling me a radical. I *am* a radical believer in God's goodness, and if you will be uncomfortable with your minister reminding you of it every week, then you will do well to beware!"

Slight laughter filtered around the room.

Everyone knew Christopher was being serious, but they appreciated his sense of humor at the same time, and his ability to point the finger at himself too.

"Well," he said, "I am also a believer in sermons that go no longer than the point of usefulness. They should be short enough to be digested and acted upon, not so long they will be ignored and forgotten. Therefore, I think I have covered all I intended today.

"Shall we pray . . ."

When he was through, everyone rose, not quite able to believe the service was already over.

It was still fifteen minutes before noon!

CHAPTER 22

LEAVING THE ROCK BY THE SIDE OF THE ROAD

The people filed out of the church, shaking Christopher's and my hands and saying all the kinds of things people say to pastors at the doors of churches. But an older man named Mr. Henry stood a few seconds in front of us after he'd shaken Christopher's hand.

"Say, I got some work fer ye, Reverend," he said, a little hesitantly. "Ain't much, maybe a couple days' worth—I'm digging me a new trench from my stream over toward the house. I wouldn't mind paying ye a fair wage to help me. This old back o' mine ain't what it used t' be."

"I'd be very appreciative, Mr. Henry," said Christopher enthusiastically. "When would you like me to start?"

"How 'bout tomorrow mornin'?"

"Couldn't be better," replied Christopher. "I'll see you over at your place bright and early."

Mr. Henry hadn't lived in Miracle Springs more than about a year. He had no wife or family and lived alone in a small place a couple of miles from town where he raised some cows and bulls. He was kind of a crusty man who kept mostly to himself, the kind of fellow little children might be afraid of. I imagined him to be fifty or fifty-five, and I didn't really know anything about him. In fact, I'm sorry to say, I'd hardly noticed him before.

Christopher went to his place the following morning and they worked all day together with shovels and picks on Mr. Henry's water line. A little before noon, Christopher told me later, Mr. Henry got real quiet for a while. They'd been talking quite a bit as they worked, and then all of a sudden Mr. Henry didn't say a word. They kept right on whacking away at the dirt and shoveling it out of the trench, but after a while Christopher started to get worried that maybe he'd said something to offend the older man. Before too much longer, though, he realized the reason for the man's silence.

"I ain't hardly been able to sleep a wink since yer last two sermons, Reverend," said Mr. Henry all at once as he tossed a shovelful of dirt aside. "I reckon I might as well just tell ye 'bout it, though it ain't the kind o' thing I ever talked about to nobody afore."

"I would be happy if you would tell me about it, Mr. Henry," said Christopher. "I promise, whatever it is, nothing you say will make me think any less of you."

"I don't reckon I'm too worried about that. It's just the kind o' thing that's hard fer a man to say, if ye know what I mean."

"I think I do."

"Well, the long an' the short o' what I'm tryin' t' git at is just this—my pa was as mean a cuss as I reckon there is, mean through and through."

As he spoke, Mr. Henry sat down on the ground, feet hanging over the edge of the trench, still holding his shovel but expending all his energy at the moment in thought.

"I don't mind tellin' ye," he went on, "when I was a kid I hated him. I know it ain't right, but I couldn't help it. So when I was listenin' to what them kin o' yers done to ye, Braxton, I knew jist what ye was talking about, 'cause my pa done worse. I thought about it all week since that story ye told 'bout when you was a kid an' how that blamed grandma an' aunt o' yers wouldn't give ye no lunch. Made me right mad, I gotta tell ye. Made me feel the same sort o' way I do when I think about my pa and what he done."

"Is your father still living, Mr. Henry?" asked Christopher, still shoveling out some loose dirt a few yards away.

"No, he's been gone fer years now. But like I said, as I was listening to ye yesterday, when ye was talking 'bout God being a father too and how we gotta not let our own past stand in the way o' being able to git ourselves right with God, something dawned on me that I never thought of afore."

"What was that?"

"Just this—that my pa's dead and gone and he lived his life good or bad, and God's gonna do with him what he wants, in the good place or the bad place. Ain't nothing I can do 'bout none o' that. That's all God's affair—ain't I right?"

"I would agree."

"The only person I can do something about is me, ain't that so?"

"That's right, Mr. Henry."

"An' I don't want the good Lord to say to me when he meets me at them pearly gates, 'Why did ye keep hanging on to all that hate so long when yer life could have been so much happier if ye'd just let go of it?' Ye think that's the kind o' thing the Lord'll say to us when we see him after we're dead?"

"I don't know, Mr. Henry. But I do certainly think it's the kind of thing he says to us now."

"So ye think it mighta been him sayin' it to me?"

"I'm sure it was."

"I reckon that's a pretty amazing thing when you stop t' think of it, that the good Lord'd say something to an' old nobody like me. And when I thought o' him asking me that question, Braxton, I got a picture in my mind o' me walking around all my life lugging a great big old rock that weighs half a ton."

He glanced over toward Christopher, then spoke again.

"That's kinda like what hate's like, would ye say?" he said.

Christopher nodded.

"And that's what I'm doing. But I don't have to, do I? I can let the blamed thing go and let it sit there by the side of the road and then I can keep going my own way."

"I like your analogy, Mr. Henry."

"Well, yer a minister, and I don't know what an analogy is. All I know is that maybe if it was the Lord putting that picture in my head, it's likely high time I got rid of this rock o' hate that's been weighing me down. And that's what I wanted to ask ye, Braxton, if you'd tell me what t' do."

"You mean about letting go of the rock?"

"Yep. I figure you said you done it—you let go o' yer rocks—so maybe you could help me git rid o' this one o' mine."

"Nothing could make me happier, Mr. Henry."

"All right then, tell me what I gotta do."

"Well, the first thing I would say is to forgive your father."

"How can I do that when he was such a mean cuss? Ain't no way around it. Forgiving him's not gonna make it go away, or make him different than he was or make it so he didn't do what he done."

"You're right. Forgiving him's not going to change a thing about what happened. All it means is that you've decided not to hold it against him anymore."

"How's that?"

"You see, when someone hurts you, nothing you do can change the fact of what they did. But you have a choice whether to hold it against them or not. If you hang on to it, then that anger remains inside you. But if you don't, then you just let it go and don't worry about what they did. That's *your* choice and doesn't really have anything to do with what the other person did at all."

"Seems like it's got *something* to do with it. If my pa hadn't been so mean to me, I wouldn't be mad at him in the first place."

"Perhaps. But you didn't *have* to get angry. Nobody made you."

"So yer sayin' I gotta stop?"

"You're the one that said you wanted to leave the rock at the side of the road. You have been holding the past against your father, but now you're going to say that you're *not* going to hold it against him anymore. It's as simple as that."

"Who do I say all that to?"

"If your father was alive, it might be good to say it to him. But since he isn't, then you say it to God, who is really your Father even more than your other father."

"What do I say?"

"Something like, 'God, I forgive my father. I'm not going to hold anything against him anymore.'"

"That's all?"

"After that you ought to ask God to forgive you."

"Forgive *me*. What fer? It was my pa who done the wrong."

"You let yourself be angry with him all these years, didn't you?"

"Yeah, I reckon so."

"That anger is the wrong that *you* did, like I said before. You didn't have to hold it against him, but you did. That was wrong of you. That was a sin both against your father and against God. That's why you have to ask forgiveness for it. That's *your* part of the wrong."

"Tarnation, Braxton, ye don't give a body much room."

"You said you wanted to let go of the rock."

"Reckon I did."

"Owning up to your *own* share of what needs forgiving is part of how to do it. Getting rid of rocks of anger like you're talking about and forgiving those who have hurt us usually has two halves to it. There aren't too many problems that only have one side to them."

Mr. Henry sat a long while pondering everything Christopher had said. Finally Christopher put down his shovel, walked over, and sat down beside him at the edge of the trench they had dug.

"Have you ever prayed before, Mr. Henry," he asked, "—out loud, as if you were talking to God like he was sitting right there on the other side of you like I am here?"

"Don't reckon I have," Mr. Henry answered.

"Would you like me to help you do that now, so you can get rid of this rock you've been lugging around all this time?"

"I reckon, but it seems a little fearsome."

"What—talking to God?"

"No, thinking that he's sitting right here with us."

"He may not be sitting here exactly like we are. But he *is* here, and we *can* talk to him just like you and I are talking. And he likes us to. He wants us to talk to him just like we're his children. He won't scold us for telling him we're sorry for what we've done. It makes him happy when we do. He's not an angry Father but a loving Father."

"I reckon I'll try it then."

"All you have to do is say something like this—'God, I forgive my father for what he did to me. I'm not going to hold it against him anymore.'"

Mr. Henry sat silent.

"Would you like to say that?"

"Uh . . . all right. Uh . . . *God, I reckon I want t' forgive my father fer what he done. I'll try not t' hold it against him no more.*"

"Good. Now say, 'And I'm sorry for being angry at my father all this time. Please forgive me.' "

"Uh, *God, I'm asking you t' forgive me fer being angry with my father.*"

"Help me to leave the rock of anger beside the road and go on without it and never pick it back up again."

"Help me t' leave the rock where it is, and not t' pick it up no more."

"Help me to be a good son to you from now on, and to call you my loving Father."

Again Mr. Henry hesitated. Christopher could tell this was the hardest thing of all for him to do—put the words *loving* and *Father* right next to each other. He waited patiently. At last Mr. Henry spoke again.

"And help me t' call you . . . to call you my loving Father," he said.

"Good, Mr. Henry. Your Father—God, that is—I am sure is very proud of you."

For the rest of that day and the next, Christopher said he had never enjoyed digging in hard ground so much!

Christopher had no work Wednesday and spent the whole day visiting people. As he said, he paid his first visit to the Gold Nugget that afternoon. Thursday he worked at the freight company, helping Marcus Weber load an order that was going down to Colfax the next day. Friday and Saturday he visited around the town some more, and by week's end neither of us had still heard a whisper from the direction of Mrs. Sinclair or any of the local gossips about where he had gone on Wednesday.

CHAPTER 23

WHAT COMPRISES FAITH?

On Christopher's second Sunday as pastor he again took the pulpit.

"Last week I said that we would talk together about the three cornerstones of Christianity as I see it," he said. "Today let us consider the second of the questions I posed: What comprises the walk of faith?

"Is faith a so-called belief system, or is it what we *do*? Do we live faith with our brains and minds . . . or with sweat and muscles, with hands and feet?"

Christopher paused and waited, but no one spoke up.

"You will probably already know the answer I intend to give," he said at length.

"I believe in the intense practicality of the Christian walk of faith. Yes, I believe faith is lived out by hands and feet during the six days of our labor, not with our brains on the Sabbath day of our rest.

"Nothing about the Christian walk of faith is abstract.

"Hear the words from Jesus' own mouth. If I can say it without seeming irreverent, how unpious they sound. They do not strike one as the words of a religious teacher, but rather a very down-to-earth and practical man. His instructions were very basic, and nearly all concerned themselves with how we are to *live*. Few of them have to do with the intellect.

"Listen to what Jesus tells us to do—lend money when asked, visit those in prison, don't envy, do good, show mercy, feed the hungry, treat others kindly, pray to your Father in heaven, speak graciously, take accountability for your actions, love your neighbor, do to others what you would like them to do to you.

"Every one of these commands is something we could walk out of this church right now . . . and *do*.

"Does a man or woman come to me with some notion concerning Christianity with no *do* attached to it? I will reply that it is not a 'Christian' thing at all—at least insofar as we presently understand it. To bring any thought or doctrine or principle under the umbrella of the Christian faith, we must find the *do-ness* of it, or else it is a dead idea that will wither and dry up and blow away in the wind.

"We must not merely find the do-ness with our brains and then satisfy ourselves that we have discovered truth. The whole purpose of our childship under the Fatherhood of God is that we *do* what the Father's children are supposed to do. That's what children do— they do as their good Father tells them.

"We have to find the practical element in *every* Christian idea principle . . . and then *do* it.

"This is called nothing more nor less than *obedience*.

"Obedience is the structural foundation of life within the Father's family. Is God truly our Father? Does he truly love us? Is he truly good and utterly to be trusted?

"What other response can there be, then, than to obey him?

"Do I want to do what I *myself* want, not what someone *else* tells me to do? Such a creed is destined to bring me misery, unhappiness, and ruin. The only pathway to fulfillment lies in willing and joyful submission to the Father's purposes, not those of our own childish fancies. Our destiny as human beings is to be his sons and daughters, not entities of our own independent making.

"Obeying him is the doorway into that destiny.

"Nor must we delay doing what God's children are to do.

"To say, 'Maybe *tomorrow* I will think about what my Father has told me to do, but today I will disregard his instructions and do what I want instead'—what can this be called other than disobedience?

"Thus, along with Christianity's practicality, I believe that there is an urgency to our obedience. Every opportunity missed is one less step on our parts toward our Father's embrace. I don't know about you, but I want with all my heart to draw close to my Father's love, not keep myself distant from it.

"In spiritual things, friends, there is no such thing as tomorrow. Every moment is *today*.

"Therefore, when your duty as a Christian, when your instructions as the Father's son or daughter, becomes clear—whether it be with regard to a principle straight from Jesus' mouth or whether it be something more personal that you feel him prompting you and you alone to do—waste not a second.

"Where is the first opportunity to *do* that thing? Go, then, and do it without delay. Then, and then only, will *life* from within that truth spring up and blossom within you."

Christopher paused, this time not to ask for questions, but to catch his breath and focus his thoughts. The congregation waited quietly.

"I said as I began these messages," he went on in a minute, "that I would be sharing the principles by which I try to order my life. This that I have just spoken, then, forms the crux of the whole. As I indicated, I do not always practice these things as successfully as I pray someday to be capable of. But if my personal creed could be reduced to a single statement, it would be this: *Spiritual truths become reality when lived.*

"These six words sum up the perspective of the man you have called to be your pastor. This is why I say, yet again—the Christian faith is practical, able to be obeyed, *do-able*, and down-to-earth . . . or it is nothing.

"So what comprises faith?

"Doing what our Father tells us. Living as he has ordained that his family lives. In other words . . . *obedience* to his commands, principles, and instructions."

Christopher paused, then added the following in conclusion.

"Now I have called Christianity a 'walk of faith,' " he said, "not a mere religion to whose tenets we mentally ascribe.

"What do I mean by *walk*?

"I mean several things. First of all, we walk with our feet, not our intellects. Faith is something we *do*, not primarily something we *think*. Walking also implies that we're going someplace. A destination exists. We're on the way somewhere. Furthermore, walking indicates a twofold process of growth. As you walk your legs get stronger and you get closer to your goal.

"In other words, being a Christian is a *process*, a journey of growth.

"The question naturally follows, what *is* it a Christian is walking toward? Are we walking toward heaven, toward the accumulation of spiritual knowledge, toward eternal rewards, toward material blessing?

"I would answer—no, it is primarily toward none of these destinations that the walk of faith is supposed to be directed. The destination is something else altogether.

"A Christian is growing and progressing toward becoming a *person* of a certain sort, a different kind of individual from the rest of the human species. This I will make my topic next week—what are we walking *toward* when we talk of walking with God?

"Let us pray . . ."

Again the service ended unexpectedly early.

CHAPTER 24

WHO'S WATCHING YOUR FAITH?

There were services at church every Sunday evening too, but from the beginning Christopher said that he would not himself speak to the people twice a day.

"I do not want to give anyone cause to tire of me," he laughed as he told this to the congregation on the evening of his first Sunday as pastor. "I will give you plenty to think about every Sunday morning and will not burden you down with more than can be digested for a week. It is my opinion that most ministers do more harm by the sheer abundance of their words than they do good with the truth contained in those words. Obedience would be far more quickly entered into by their people if all the sermons of the world's clergymen were immediately cut in half—including my own."

"Amen, Reverend!" called out Uncle Nick, and everyone laughed, Christopher along with them.

"If my words begin to bore any one of you at any time," he went on, "I beg you to tell me, and I will take my seat immediately!"

He paused, smiling, while everyone settled back into a more serious mood.

"In the meantime," Christopher continued after a moment, "on Sunday evenings I intend to hear from *you*. We will sing, perhaps more than during the morning service, and we will share together how we are learning to trust God in our lives and how we are learning to call him Father. In other words, I will call upon *you* to share and speak and lead the evening services. If we are to have

125

an active and growing ministry in this church, it will be because we are involved in it together as an entire community."

That first Sunday evening, we just sang and prayed and a few people shared informally right from their seats—mostly remembrances of Rev. Rutledge, as well as saying how happy they were that Christopher and I were staying in Miracle Springs to take his place.

On Tuesday of the following week, Christopher asked Pa if he'd speak the next time.

"*Me*—preach a sermon?" exclaimed Pa.

"No," replied Christopher. "The last thing I want from you, Drum, is a sermon. I just want you to share informally. Everyone in this community looks up to you and respects you."

"What do you want me to talk about?"

"Whatever you like—what it means to you that you're a Christian, how you try to live out your Christianity."

"I'd have to give it some thought, but I reckon I could do that," said Pa.

"Sure you can. Anyone who can get up and speak in front of the California legislature can speak to a few dozen of his friends."

"That was a long time ago."

"All the more reason. You're older and wiser now."

"Yeah—says who?" laughed Pa.

But Pa did what Christopher asked, and the next Sunday evening he told the folks of Miracle Springs about his first meeting with Avery Rutledge, how he'd been antagonistic to spiritual things to begin with, but how he and Rev. Rutledge had eventually become good friends and helped build the church together.

"A lot of you weren't here back then," Pa said, "so I figured you might like to hear about that. It's a lesson that's always stuck with me all these years. Preachers come in all sizes and shapes, just like everyone else. Avery Rutledge, I reckon, was about as different a fellow as there could be from my son-in-law. At first I didn't think I liked him all that well, as I told you—Avery, that is, son," he added, glancing over with a smile toward Christopher. "But he was a man that lived his faith, and that made all the difference. A man who lives what he believes—that's a powerful man, 'cause people take notice of that, and sometimes it can't help changing them, like it did me.

"That's why I know Christopher's exactly right with all he's been telling us about us needing to *do* what we say we believe. Because if I hadn't seen a man doing what *he* said he believed, I wouldn't be standing up here in front of you tonight. It's that *doing* that makes it come alive for whoever's watching. So listen to what he says. And then pay attention to your *do*, 'cause you never know who's watching your life like I was Avery's. Why, somebody's watching me right now . . . and somebody's no doubt watching you too. Might be somebody we don't even know. But there might be someone standing up speaking their mind in this very church five or ten years from now, telling about how they're walking with God because of what they saw in your life just this last week, or maybe next.

"I reckon that's a pretty sobering thought. To be honest with you, it kinda scares me a little. I ain't even sure I like it. But I don't suppose it can be helped. I looked at Avery and I saw something. Our old friend Alkali Jones was watching me, though I never knew it, and when he prayed with Christopher here to be one of the Lord's men before he died, he told him so, and I tell you it downright flabbergasted me. So whether I like it or not, I can see that's how it works."

He paused briefly. "When people are trying to be Christians," he added, "other folks watch—that's all there is to it. So we better pay attention to what we're about."

Pa stopped again, and this time glanced around, suddenly aware, I think, that he was starting to sound a little like a preacher himself!

"Well, I reckon I better heed what Christopher said last week," said Pa, "and cut this here sermon in half!"

Christopher stood, came up front laughing, shook Pa's hand and thanked him, and Pa sat down next to Almeda.

"Maybe Corrie and I should have gone to Virginia after all," said Christopher. "It looks like you had a preacher in your midst and didn't even know it!"

The following Sunday evening, Christopher talked Mr. Henry into sharing with the church about their conversation on anger and leaving the rock beside the road. He didn't want to at first, but eventually he agreed. And after that, whenever he could, Christopher had one of the other men—and sometimes women too—of the community to speak or share. After Pa's and Mr. Henry's example, most were willing to tell a little or a lot about what God was doing in their lives.

CHAPTER 25

A LETTER

An unexpected letter came a week or so later—about three weeks after our decision to stay in California.

A *really* unexpected letter!

It began,

> *Dear Cornelia and Christopher,*
> *I am sure I am the last person on earth you will expect to hear from.*

We quickly turned to the second page to see who the letter was from, and he was right—I was surprised!

> *I am writing from the Sacramento jail, where I had the good fortune to share a cell with your friend Jesse Harris. He told me all about the time he spent in Miracle Springs, how he went there intent on killing your father and instead became friends with your family. He told me how much your family did for him. And he talks about what he describes as a clean new feeling in his soul from forgiving and being forgiven, and giving himself to God for the rest of his life.*
> *It is like nothing I ever heard before, though now remembering some of our past conversations, Cornelia, I realize that you tried to tell me about God years ago, but I was so selfish and scheming that I never heard what you were really saying. I suppose it takes a run of bad luck sometimes to wake you up to how things really are and to get you to look at the truth as it really is. I guess that's what happened to me. I*

want you to know that I'm a changed man now.

About a year ago I got myself mixed up with some land swindlers about fifty miles south of here. I didn't know what they were up to, but was just looking to make a few easy dollars, so I agreed to operate their office front in Stockton— which was just for show—while they went out and made the deals. When the thing went sour they disappeared, and there I was in the office looking like it was my scheme all along because they'd gotten me to sign the lease on the office in my own name. I had been framed for the whole thing. Trying to explain things to two federal marshals, I saw immediately how stupid I had been, but it was too late. I've been in jail now for two months waiting for my trial, and with no money to put up for bail.

These last two months sitting here searching my own soul, and then talking with Jesse—well, the long and the short of it is that I've decided to give whatever's left of my life to God too. Jesse's told me what to say and how to pray, just like he did, and I feel a lot better already. I only wish I'd have listened to you earlier, Cornelia, and not acted like such a fool. I'm sure sorry for all the things I did and said to you through the years, and for the way I behaved in San Francisco last year. I want you to know that I'm a changed man.

I'm hesitant to ask, but Jesse says that the two of you are the kind of people who will help anybody, and he told me I shouldn't be afraid to write you. So I decided to take his advice and write and ask if you might consider helping me put up the two hundred dollars in bail money. I know it's a lot to ask. But my trial isn't for three more months, and I know if I could get out, I might be able to find out something of where the men are who got me into all this, which the lawyer says would really help me. You'd get it all back, of course, at the trial. But I'll understand if you can't.

Well, that's about all I have to say, except that I'm sorry again, and thank you for what you did for Jesse, who passed it on to me.

Yours sincerely,
Robert O'Flaridy

I let the two sheets drop from my hand with a sigh of so many different feelings, I hardly knew what to think. Christopher and I were both silent a long minute or two. Robert, whom I had known for fifteen years as Robin O'Flaridy—we'd both worked years ago for the same San Francisco newspaper—and who had pulled so many tricks and shenanigans on me I couldn't remember them all, was the *last* person I'd have expected to hear news like this from.

"I just can't believe it," I said finally.

"It is exactly as your father said," added Christopher, "somebody's always watching. And now we come to find out that even Robin O'Flaridy was paying more attention than you thought."

"It's . . . it's just so hard to imagine," I said again. "He was just the same as always when we saw him last May."

"Nobody is outside God's love," said Christopher, "even those we least expect to be attentive to his voice."

"What should we do?" I asked.

"It hardly seems coincidental that this comes right after I've been telling the people about the practicality of the Christian faith. So much from my last week's sermon comes right back into my mind. Do you remember what I said Jesus told us to do—lend money when asked, do good, visit those in prison?"

"But doesn't this seem a lot like that woman in St. Louis?" I asked, wanting to believe the best, yet still hesitant. "The one who took your money after you tried to help her?"

"But this is completely different," rejoined Christopher. "This is someone you know. That woman was a stranger and a con artist."

"Yes, and I've been conned by Robin before."

Christopher nodded and it fell silent. I knew he was trying to weigh his own feelings with what I'd said, and trying somehow to balance the two sides.

"So you think we ought to do it?" I asked finally.

"What else can this be," sighed Christopher, "but the Lord's way of giving *us* the opportunity to see if we really mean what I've been speaking about? If *we* don't obey his words when we have the chance, how can I expect the rest of the congregation to?"

"Do we even have two hundred dollars?" I asked.

"I think we have just about that much left in the bank from my share of the mining work."

"What about the tithe fund?"

"No," Christopher replied, "that can only be used for the people of our community."

We both fell to thinking again for a minute or two.

"What do you think you'll do?" I asked finally.

"I suppose I could wire the money down to the capital," replied Christopher. "But I think I probably ought to combine both those two commands—lend when asked and visit those in prison. I think I should take the train down there and see to the matter personally."

"You could visit Jesse too," I suggested.

"Would you want to come with me?"

"I'm not sure I'm up to a visit with Robin O'Flaridy quite yet," I replied, "even if he has become a Christian. That may take me a little time to get used to."

CHAPTER 26

WHAT IS GOD'S PURPOSE?

Two days later Christopher left for Sacramento.

He didn't want to be gone over the weekend and had originally planned to wait until Monday. Then he was reminded of his words about the urgency of obedience and so decided to take the very next train. He asked Pa and Almeda and me and Mr. Shaw to take care of the Sunday services. He told us it was all right if we did a lot of hymn singing and said that Harriet Rutledge would be happy to help us with anything.

He arrived back in Miracle Springs the following Tuesday, a little subdued it seemed to me.

"How's Jesse?" I asked.

"He's doing very well. Still not much news about his future, but his spirits are good, and he's telling everyone he meets about the Lord."

"And Robin?"

"Yes, I saw him too. He's fine. Seemed a lot different than the last time I saw him."

"You put up his bail?"

Christopher nodded.

I decided to ask no more questions for the moment. Christopher didn't seem in a very talkative mood. I imagined he was tired from his trip.

By the following Sunday he was back to his old energetic self. When that day came, once again he took his place in front of the Miracle Springs congregation to finish the last of the series he'd been doing, which had now been delayed a week.

"We have been considering together what I call my cornerstones of belief," Christopher began. "In my mind, and in my life's experience, they form a progression, a progression which I believe growing Christians must go through. Not just pastors who think about such things—but all who consider themselves Christians. Though some theologians may disagree with me, I do not find this progression optional. I believe that to grow, one *must* go through each of its successive stages.

"First, we must discover what God's character is like.

"Sad to say, many Christians never really make this discovery, and as a result they live their lives fearing God's wrath rather than learning to trust his goodness. Thus they are unable to grow in their relationship with him, because they are not acquainted with his true personality. How many of you would say you were on intimate terms with me, for example, if you had no idea what kind of person I was? And yet we so easily make that same mistake with God.

"Once we are acquainted with God as our Father, the second stage of the progression, which we considered two weeks ago, is learning to walk with him in daily faith.

"Today we will look at the third and final aspect of this progression—toward what are we walking?"

Christopher paused and took a couple of breaths.

"The question we now want to consider," he began again, "is this: *What is God's purpose in our lives?* What is it he desires to accomplish? Toward what is faith supposed to point?

"We now find ourselves at what, for me, represents the third cornerstone of belief. And it is just this—I believe that the objective toward which the Father is guiding and leading his sons and daughters, that which he is 'growing' us to become, is nothing less than Christlikeness of character.

"If we are living trees, that is the fruit the species called mankind is supposed to produce. If we are flowers, that is the blossom that is the end result of being—*Christlikeness*."

He paused again to let his words sink in.

"That is why it matters so little in one way what we say with our mouths and what we believe in our brains about the many doctrines of the Christian religion. What matters is this: *What kind of people does our Christian walk cause us to become?*

"Are we becoming more like Jesus? Then *truly* we are walking the Christian faith!

"Will any of us ever *achieve* Christlikeness of character in this life?" Christopher asked, looking around at us all. "Will we ever fully manifest that fruit on our character-trees? Of course not.

"We can, however, with each passing year, be walking upward on the road of faith so that, though imperfect, Christlikeness will slowly become more evident in our attitudes and our characters. The fruit of Christlikeness *can* grow on these trees of ours, even in spite of the human limitations of imperfection. Not every apple on an apple tree is what we might call a *perfect* apple. But they're all apples, as different as every one might be . . . and they all make great apple pies.

"Such is the goal. This is what ought to define what we call 'a Christian life.' "

CHAPTER 27

HOW IS IT ACHIEVED?

Christopher paused, while some shifting sounds went around the church.

"Now let me ask one of the most important questions of all," he went on. "How does this growth I am speaking of come about? How *does* the Father cause the character of his firstborn son, who is Jesus, to be infused into the characters of all those others who choose to become his sons and daughters?

"It is very simple really. Simple, that is, considering what a high thing it is we are considering.

"I believe that as we do what the Father and Jesus have instructed, the Holy Spirit causes a change toward Christlikeness to take place within us. As we gradually slice off bits and pieces of our selfish self—what is called the flesh or the old man—the Father replaces them with tiny infusions of Jesus' character.

"But that raises a question: Does Christlikeness come about by *God's* doing or *our* doing?"

Christopher watched as everyone thought about his or her answer.

"Both," he said after a moment. "God has given instructions about how his people are to live. As *we* practice and obey those instructions, by the choices we make and by our own determination to put others first, then *he* causes the change to happen—over the course of many weeks, months, and years. Increasingly, we respond to people, situations, and events more as Jesus himself would respond. It is not easy to do so. But with practice we gradually learn. And then the transformation comes as we do what Jesus has told us to do."

Christopher paused, thought a moment, then smiled.

"Let me give you an example," he said. "You come in after a long, hard day's work with dirt all over your hands—just like Mr. Henry and I looked by the time we were finished with his trench! Now, you go to the basin and pick up the bar of soap with one hand. But your other hand is tied behind your back, so you have to try to wash your one free hand all by itself."

A few chuckles went around.

"Try it when you get home!" laughed Christopher. "It's not so easy. It works a lot better when you get *both* hands into the water with that bar of soap!

"That's exactly how the Christian life works. We can't do it alone without the Lord's help. But neither can he do much in the way of growing the kind of fruit he's trying to grow in us by *himself*, without *our* help. God's part and ours go hand in hand. You can't separate them.

"The more times you are kind or forgiving to someone who is mean to you, the more capable you become of responding like Jesus. You become a kinder and more forgiving person. The Holy Spirit working inside you may be causing the change to happen, but *you* are the one who makes it possible by repeated kind and forgiving actions that *you* do yourself.

"God cannot do this without our help. *'Father, make me to become like Jesus,'* is a worthy prayer. It is, in fact, one of the highest prayers possible for a man or woman to pray. But God cannot answer it unless we are doing what he tells us to do—being kind and forgiving and doing to others as we would have them do to us.

"It is from obedience that this transformation I speak of comes. That's both hands working together.

"Therefore, we must know what we have been told to do and what kind of people the children of God are to be. In order to make this possible, it is urgent and imperative that we know what the New Testament teaches. Not so that we will merely *know* it, but so that we will know what it is we are supposed to *do*.

"In the New Testament are our instructions, our orders, to be found. The Gospels are most important of all. If we hope to become like him, *we have to do what Jesus said!*

"If Drum or Almeda were going to hire someone to manage the freight company who knew nothing about the business, they would first give him detailed instructions. They might even write down a list of all his duties. Then they would expect him to do everything they had instructed.

"As Christians we too have been left with instructions.

"The four Gospels are our guidebook. They tell us how we are supposed to live, what our attitudes should be, how we are to behave, how we are to think, what we should do in various situations. Familiarity with the Gospels is foundational if you and I hope to make progress on our walks of faith toward becoming like Jesus.

"When we do read our Bibles, there are many topics that can be raised for discussion. We can talk about salvation, we can talk about God's mercy and grace, we can talk about what Paul calls justification, we can examine the prophetic portions of Scripture, we can try to describe exactly what faith is, we can discuss the afterlife.

"There are a multitude of doctrines and qualities of God's being upon which theologians hang their opinions like coats on a row of pegs. Every coat looks a little different, and after a while the wall is so cluttered with coats that you no longer see the pegs. When I was in seminary I studied most of the theological pegs, so to speak, but I found myself none the wiser for it.

"I thus determined within myself that I would search the Scriptures to find what for me seemed the essential points which I myself believed to comprise the Christian faith. These I am sharing with you now. Open any page of the New Testament, point out any verse on any topic, and the truths therein will reduce, in the final analysis, to these cornerstone principles of belief I have been sharing with you.

"Who is God and what is his character?

"What comprises the walk of faith?

"What is God's ultimate purpose in our lives?

"Those three questions may be found, as I say, on every page of the Scriptures—if only we learn to discover and discern them.

"There is not a single attribute of God, nor a single doctrine about his work, his plan, or his creation in which God's good, loving, and trustworthy Fatherhood cannot be found. We could list fifty things that God 'is,' but they would all merely describe the fact that he is our Father. We could list a hundred things that God 'does,' but they would all be mere corollaries to his love, goodness, and trustworthiness.

"In the same way, there is not a single verse in the New Testament that does not contain a practical element, a call to God's children to grow into Christlikeness by the obedient living out of self-denial and servanthood.

"Open the Bible to any page, read any sentence, and there, if you have eyes to see, you will find practicality, Christlikeness, and relinquishment of self—with the Fatherhood of God overarching the whole.

"It took some time, and I had to retrain myself to read my Bible through eyes that could perceive these three cornerstones and the principles involved in living them. You can imagine the difficulty of a former seminarian such as myself, who had studied under theologians with more letters *after* their names than my name contains, of putting aside doctrines, opinions, and ideas and seeking instead nothing from the holy Scriptures other than what I was to *do* in the next five minutes.

"But I did learn to retrain myself, to adjust my brain to see the New Testament not as a religious treatise full of ideas, but as the most practical guidebook about living the world has ever been given. As we study the Scriptures together while I am your pastor, it will be with just such a practical focus."

CHAPTER 28

WHAT IS CHRISTLIKENESS?

Christopher paused momentarily, glanced down at his watch, then thought for a moment.

"It is about ten minutes till noon," he said. "I had planned to stop there. Yet it somehow seems to me appropriate to continue just a few minutes longer in order to ask, and then answer, one more extremely vital question. What exactly do I mean, some of you may find yourselves wondering, when I speak of this thing called *Christlikeness*? I would not have you leave this morning with that question unanswered in your mind."

Christopher drew in a breath.

"Whenever someone comes to me," he went on, "though the occasions have not been many since I left my last church, with the question, 'What must I do to become a Christian?' my answer is always, 'Give yourself fully—intellect, hands, feet, heart, brain, thoughts, feelings, attitudes, behavior—to your heavenly Father who loves you. Ask him to forgive you for trying to live independent from him and to forgive your sins—which he happily does. You may become his son or daughter simply by asking him to take you into his family, by *giving* yourself to him.'

"The question that usually comes next is: 'What do I do then?' My reply always is, 'Read the Gospels. Find out what Jesus taught. He is the example of how a child of the Father is to live. Do what he says, therefore, and model your life after his. That is how life is lived within the Father's family.' In other words, once we allow God to forgive us, and once Jesus' death and blood wash us clean, then we *are* part of God's family. Then we must *live* as his children live.

"That *is* the Christian life—doing as Jesus did, living the life of God's family.

"But one might inquire further: 'What, at its essential core, does it mean to do as Jesus did? What defines the Christlike character?'

"I will answer by saying that in sacrifice, self-denial, servanthood, and death of self-motive is to be found the abundant life which the Father longs to lavish forth upon his children without measure. For such attributes made up the moment-by-moment life of God's Son.

"Everything in God's kingdom is inverted from the ways of man.

"Man says, 'Get all you can and you will be happy.' God says, '*Give* what you have, and you will have riches indeed.'

"Man says, 'Raise yourself up.' God says, 'Put your self to *death.*'

"Man says, 'The greatest goal is to possess.' God says, 'The highest ambition in life is to *relinquish.*'

"Man says, 'To be served by others is to be great.' God says, 'Greatness is measured by *servanthood.*'

"Man says, 'The first are first and the last are last.' God says, '*The last shall be first, and the first last.*'

"Jesus rose to the height of his sonship by willingly laying down his life. Why did he do so? To teach us how to lay down our own selfishness, and in order that his Father's purposes might be fulfilled. He never sought his own will, only his Father's.

"As he is our example, only in so doing will we—you and I, my friends—reach the height of our sonship and daughterhood within the Father's family . . . by laying down everything that we might otherwise call our own.

"Now please don't get me wrong. This may not necessarily involve the actual giving of one's earthly life. That is something that comes to very few. But the opportunity to do what I am speaking of comes to *everyone.* More than that, it comes to us every day.

"I am speaking rather of laying down, of denying, of putting to death, our natural motives of self, responding to every situation that crosses our path with the automatic silent inward question,

How may I be a servant to this other individual? What sacrifice can I make that will help him in some way? What can I say or do—what good can I do, what kindness can I show, what gracious word can escape my lips—that will convey my Father's love to this dear one whom the Father has put before me?

"Laying down our lives means nothing more nor nothing less than simply putting others ahead of ourselves—giving their needs and desires preeminence over our own. It means stepping to the back of the line and letting others go first. It means washing other people's feet rather than expecting them to wash ours.

"Such was, it is my firm conviction, how Jesus lived every moment of his life. He possessed no motive of self. His only desire was to do his *Father's* will.

"If he is our example, then surely we are to do the same."

Christopher stopped and took in a deep breath, then wiped his forehead with his handkerchief. Every eye was fixed on him and there wasn't a sound in the whole church.

When he spoke again his voice was quieter, yet just as firm. I could tell he was nearly done.

"Is this remarkable life of dynamic and practical Christlike Christianity," he asked, "—is it meant for only a few, for especially 'religious' individuals, for pious older men and women, for monks in a monastery or nuns in a convent?

"Is it meant only for pastors, perhaps such as Avery Rutledge and myself, and maybe also for our wives, but not for working men and women who have to exist in the real world facing the sorts of struggles and strains that we clerics do not have to?

"Is it somehow *easier* for someone such as myself because I happen to be called a pastor?

"Is the life of Christlikeness reserved only for church time on Sundays?

"What do you think of all this I have been saying? Is there anything here . . . for *you*?

"Well, my friends, I will close with my final point—and it is perhaps the most important of all.

"I believe that the life of self-denial, servanthood, and obedient Christlikeness is the destiny and calling of *every* man and woman who calls himself or herself a Christian. That means every one of you listening to me here today.

"It is to such a life as I have been describing, as I told you some weeks ago, that I will challenge you every Sunday, and every day during the week between Sundays. Consider the challenge carefully. This is the life *all* Christians are called to live—not pastors only."

Christopher paused, then added with a sincere smile, "But that's where the pastor comes in—to make the challenge, and to help you however I can to live this life of Christlikeness.

"Let me say once again how thankful I am to be living among you. My wife and I love you all dearly. Let us conclude in prayer together.

"Father, we are grateful that you love us and that you call us your children. Help us to be more fully the sons and daughters we are. Help us to live obediently to your will. Transform us, each and every one, into people who reflect the character of your Son, Jesus. Go with us as we return to our homes, and keep us mindful of you every day in the week which follows. Thank you, Father. Amen."

As Christopher opened his eyes, he nodded down to me where I sat. I stood, took his arm, and we walked down the center aisle together toward the door of the church.

CHAPTER 29

SHOCKING SURPRISE

I was learning real quick that the life of a pastor was more involved than I'd ever dreamed. It wasn't long before I began to see what hard work pastoring could be. I didn't see how Christopher could keep up with his work schedule and his visiting schedule, because for me the latter was just as taxing as the former. Within a couple of months I was starting to get tired—I mean physically *tired*—by the end of every day.

It seemed like everyone needed to try out the new pastor with this problem, that problem, this issue, that issue. Then would come a family crisis, an illness, a conflict, a situation in town, financial difficulties, misunderstandings, and even a few criticisms that came Christopher's way from unnamed sources—day in and day out, it all took its toll on me.

Christopher said it was all part of the ministry and that teaching spiritual principles on Sunday morning was only one very small portion of the whole. Occasionally the misunderstandings and difficulties with people got him down, but all the rest of it seemed to exhilarate him, as if he thrived on being part of men's and women's lives at such a level. But as for me—like I said, it wore me out.

I found myself beginning to wonder if I was cut out to be a minister's wife at all! I was used to having time to write and think and read. And I was used to having more time just with Christopher, but now overnight our lives hardly seemed like our own anymore.

Two things happened around the beginning of that summer of 1868 involving two people I had known for as long as I'd been in California, which was now over half my life. They were two very opposite things—one good and one bad, one that put Christopher into a deeper pit of discouragement and self-doubt than I'd ever seen him in, and the other that confirmed to him more than ever that we'd made the right decision in staying in California. I'll tell you about them in the order they came, which was the disheartening one first, followed by the encouraging one a week later.

The time arrived for Robin O'Flaridy's trial. When they'd visited earlier, Christopher had promised to return for the trial so that he might put in a good word for Robin if possible. By this time Christopher had talked me into returning to Sacramento with him.

We had a good time on the train ride down. It was so nice to get away from Miracle Springs for two or three days and just be alone together. We talked and talked again, like we really hadn't had a chance to in months. Already we were learning that being involved with people can't help but change a man and woman's relationship. They have to share one another with everyone else, and that makes it hard to keep communicating on the same level as when there was only the two of them.

The closer to Sacramento we got, the more I found my thoughts turning to Robin O'Flaridy, and I began telling Christopher so many of the old stories about the shenanigans he had pulled and how I'd tried so hard to get through to him about a different way of living than always trying to dupe someone.

"I am so glad he's finally changed," I said. "To be honest, I never thought he would. He was such a dyed-in-the-wool conniver!"

I couldn't help laughing as I thought of how he had stolen my idea and scooped me on the Miracle Springs mayor's election between Almeda and Mr. Royce.

"Maybe finally we can genuinely help him," I added. "I always thought he had great potential to really be someone."

When we arrived in the capital, we first went to the jail to visit Mr. Harris. He was so happy to see us and seemed to be doing wonderfully. His trial had finally been scheduled for about a month from then, and he said the way it looked he would only have to spend a year or two in prison.

That evening we went out to dinner, then back to the boarding house. The following morning at nine o'clock we went to the courthouse for Robin's trial. We sat down in the visitors' gallery and waited.

Christopher had briefly met one or two of the attorneys involved in the case when he was in the city earlier to post bail, so he recognized the man who approached us, with one of the court bailiffs alongside him, a few minutes after nine. Christopher stood and the two men shook hands.

"Have you seen your friend O'Flaridy?" the man asked.

"No, not since I was here several months ago," replied Christopher. "We just came down yesterday . . . for the trial. Why, is there—?"

"A problem? Indeed there is. It seems your friend has jumped bail and is nowhere to be found."

Christopher's face turned white.

"I . . . I don't believe it. I was sure—"

"Believe it, Mr. Braxton," rejoined the attorney. "I've seen his kind more than I can tell you. You get so you can tell. He's gone."

"What . . . what does it mean now?" asked Christopher.

"It means, first of all, that you'll never see your two hundred dollars again. It also means that you're now more involved than you probably intended to be. That's why the bailiff is here. He's going to have to take you to the judge. I'm afraid you've got some explaining to do over *your* role in this thing."

"Come along, Mr. Braxton," now said the bailiff, taking hold of Christopher's arm—a little rudely, I thought. I was too frightened to be angry, but they didn't need to treat him like a criminal! But before I had a chance even to think about it, Christopher was being led away, and soon he had disappeared through a door with the bailiff, two attorneys, and the judge. I sat there I think as scared as I've ever been in my life. Some horrible premonition kept telling me the next time I saw my husband he was going to be wearing handcuffs and be on his own way to jail!

Fortunately, it was not a premonition based in fact. About ten minutes later Christopher reappeared through the same door, face still ashen and visibly shaken. Whatever the judge had said had obviously not been pleasant.

He came back up the aisle toward me, paused, gave me his hand without any change in his expression, and we left the courtroom in silence. Maybe it was just my imagination, but it felt like every eye was upon us.

Once we were outside the courtroom, Christopher said, "I had a bad feeling about it after I talked to Robin when I came down here before, but I didn't want to face it."

"What kind of feeling?" I asked.

"A nervousness that maybe he wasn't being completely truthful with me. I guess I should have listened to my reservations."

"There was no way you could have known."

Christopher just sighed. "Let's get out of here," he said, "and go home!"

CHAPTER 30

HARD QUESTIONS

We were back on the northbound train within two hours, during which time Christopher hardly said two dozen words. I'd never seen him like this—so low and despondent, as if he singlehandedly had caused the collapse of the entire justice system of the United States of America. I kept trying to tell him that it wasn't his fault and wasn't even as bad as it might seem.

"When the judge started talking about my being an accomplice in the whole scheme," Christopher sighed, "I didn't exactly feel as if it wasn't my fault."

"You—an accomplice!" I exclaimed. "How could they think such a thing?"

"You've got to admit it doesn't look good."

"If you were in on it, why would you come back?"

"One of the attorneys pointed that out to him. But he was talking about bringing charges against me anyway, until the attorney reminded him I was a minister and had only been trying to help. Then the judge laughed—and that was worse. 'A fake conversion to weasel bail money out of a parson,' he said. 'I've seen it so many times. You religious fellows are sitting ducks for their kind!' "

Poor Christopher! His voice was so forlorn as he told me of the painful interview.

"Don't you understand, Corrie?" was all he kept saying, "I gave my word. It wasn't just two hundred dollars, although that's bad enough—we can hardly afford to lose that kind of money. But it was a pledge that Robin would be there. It was my guarantee—

that is how the court looks at it. I was honor bound to make sure he appeared. It . . . it just never *dawned* on me," he added for what must have been the tenth time, "that he wouldn't be there. I had the feeling he wasn't telling me everything . . . but I never dreamed he would just run away."

His voice and whole expression was so full of disbelief that someone, even someone like Robin T. O'Flaridy, would *not* do what he said. The thing struck him as categorically impossible. How *could* truth be so violated? It was as if his brain could not contain the idea of not doing what one promised.

The first half of the train ride was almost silent. Nothing I could say or do could console poor Christopher. I even began to wonder if he was mad at me for some reason, though I kept telling myself that couldn't be so.

"Do you know what's the worst of it of all?" he said suddenly after we had bounced along for probably thirty entire minutes of silence. "It's not being used and taken advantage of so much. It's not even losing all that money. The Lord will make it back up, and it's his money anyway. But what makes it so hard is for things like this to happen when you're honestly and sincerely trying to *help* people. If I was selfish, if I was mean, if I was out for myself—that would be one thing. But I honestly do want to do good for others, Corrie. I really do."

"I know, Christopher. And God sees that desire in your heart."

"But why doesn't anyone else?"

"I do."

Christopher nodded, then placed his hand on mine.

"And so do lots of people," I added. "Why else do you think the community wanted you as its pastor? Why else does my family love you so much? Everyone who really knows you recognizes that about you—that you live for others."

Christopher sighed. I thought I'd never seen someone so dejected.

"I thought I was somewhat discriminating," he said. "I thought I knew people. But I can't trust myself. Where's my discernment? It's no different than that lady in St. Louis. I think I'm trying to help people, but I'm just a gullible fool."

"That's one of the reasons I love you," I said softly.

"What—that I'm a gullible fool?"

"No, that you're always trying to help people."

"But what good do I really do anyone? This kind of thing seems to happen over and over. You'd think someone with my background would be more naturally suspicious of people. As ill-treated as I was, you'd think I'd have a healthy, sober-mindedness about people and their motives. I'm beginning to think a little mistrust might be good in my case!"

"You don't really mean that."

"I haven't even told you about the Draws family back in Richmond. I don't *want* to tell you—it's too painful to remember all I tried to do for them, and what happened in the end."

"Maybe that's one of the chances you take when you try to help others."

"It seems like it ought to turn out differently."

"Jesus said to give, and you obeyed. You were trying to do right."

"And look what's come of it?"

"It hasn't hurt us. We've only lost some money."

"Almost all we had in the bank! And what good have we done Robin? We've just allowed him one more successful con. How does this help him see his need of the Lord? And besides all that, what can the truth of the gospel look like to those men back there who think I'm just a foolish pastor without an ounce of brains."

"We were trying to do what we thought was right. I know what it looks like to you now, but I can't help it, Christopher—I hope we always do that."

CHAPTER 31

AN UNEXPECTED CALLER ON A MORE UNEXPECTED ERRAND

It was the middle of the following week when Mr. Royce the banker came out to the house for a call none of us would ever forget. Christopher was more like his old self again by then, though I could tell the O'Flaridy incident was still weighing on his confidence.

Mr. Royce came mostly to see Pa, but when he found out that Christopher was there too, he asked if he could talk to both of them together. It was obviously intended to be a talk between men, so Christopher and Pa took Mr. Royce into our little bunkhouse home, and I went into the big house.

Christopher told me about it that evening.

"I've been needing to talk to you for a long time, Mr. Hollister," Mr. Royce began.

"Please, Franklin," Pa stopped him. "I thought we were past those formalities a long time ago. You gotta call me Drum."

"All right, er . . . Drum," replied Mr. Royce. "I'll try." He paused to clear his throat nervously. Christopher said he'd never seen a man so nervous, which, the way I'd known Mr. Royce from years past, really was unusual. I could hardly imagine it even though Christopher was telling me every detail.

"Go on . . . go on, Franklin," Pa tried to encourage him. "You're among friends here."

Mr. Royce nodded his head, then did his best to get what he'd come for out of his mouth.

"I suppose I knew this day would have to come sooner or later, Hollis—, er . . . uh, Drum. You and I've had our differences over the years—"

"Long time ago, Franklin," interrupted Pa again. "No hard feelin's on my end, that's for sure, and I can tell you the same's true for Almeda, and that's a fact."

"I believe you, Drum. It is because I know what you say is true that I'm here. You're a man of your word. Everyone knows that, and, it may surprise you to learn, I know it too."

Pa nodded in grateful acknowledgment but did not reply.

"You see, I've been watching you, Drummond Hollister," Mr. Royce continued. "I've been watching you all these years without even knowing I *was* watching you. Somehow, even in the midst of some pretty rough differences we had, I knew you bore me no malice. You got angry with me a time or two, but I deserved it. You gave me a pretty sound thrashing that day in my office. But I deserved worse than the bloody nose and bruised jaw you gave me. Yours was the right kind of anger for a man to have, but mine was purely selfish. Even when you went into business against me, down inside—though I was furious at you—I knew you were only doing it to help people whose needs I was too selfish to see."

I couldn't believe what Christopher was telling me! Franklin Royce, the slick and shrewd banker, was the last person I ever expected to be saying such things!

"I resented you, Drummond. I resented your beating me in the mayor's election, I resented how you saved your friends from my foreclosures, I resented that everyone looked up to you, I resented that Miracle Springs' most beautiful woman fell in love with you, and I resented your success and reputation in the high political circles of Sacramento. Most of all, I resented the simple fact that everyone liked you, while I know they didn't like me."

"Aw, you're being too hard on yourself, Franklin," said Pa. "Folks maybe don't show it like they should, but they like you just like—"

"That's another thing I know about you, Drummond," interrupted Mr. Royce this time. "You're a terrible liar. You once called me a liar, and you were speaking the truth. But you're too honest a man for it yourself. I doubt if you could tell a lie if you had to, so let me continue before you attempt to go any further with the one you just started."

Pa was quiet. Christopher watched both men, almost wondering why he was there with them. Yet it was wonderful to behold at the same time, and he never thought of leaving.

"I'm ashamed to say all this," Mr. Royce continued, "but I'm finally beginning to see some things clearly that I should have seen years ago. The main thing I am seeing is the very thing that's been right in front of my eyes all this time, but which I was too blinded by resentment and my own pride and anger to see. That is the simple fact that you, Drummond Hollister, are a good and unselfish man."

Even as the words were coming out of his mouth, Christopher said that Mr. Royce could tell that Pa was getting ready to interrupt him again. So he put up his hands before Pa could say a word and kept right on talking.

"I know, I know," he said, "that you're no saint and that you've had troubles with the law and that you spent some years doing things you probably wish you hadn't. But that doesn't take anything away from the fact that ever since I've known you at least, you've been trying to do good to your neighbor, and that even includes me. You'd have done anything for me in a second if I'd have let you, wouldn't you have?"

" 'Course I would, Franklin," replied Pa, softly and seriously. He was deeply moved by what Mr. Royce was saying.

"Now I knew that when you and your kids got back together, and when the Rev. Rutledge came, and then when you and Almeda got married, I knew you were spending more time in the church. There was talk about town about Hollister 'gettin' religion,' but inside I scoffed at it. I knew what you were up to. I knew that it was all just a ploy to get your hands on Almeda's money. Even after you invited me to your home for Christmas dinner that year, though it became civil between us, down inside I still resented you.

"Do you see . . . do you see what a snake I've been, and why I had to come talk to you? Like I said, I was watching—watching it all. I was watching to see, secretly hoping you'd go out and get drunk or be found with another woman or get caught with your hand in the till of the Mine and Freight Company. I wanted people to see that you were a phony and a hypocrite."

Mr. Royce stopped and looked away, obviously full of emotion.

"I am ashamed of myself for saying so, but that is how I felt. But you disappointed me, Drummond. Because you *weren't* a phony. Whatever kind of religion you found, it was obviously real and important to you. I could see you were a different kind of person than I was. Oh, I went to church like all the other respectable citizens of Miracle Springs. I had to. I am a businessman and must watch my reputation. I must be upstanding in people's eyes.

"So I sat in church with you and the others. But you were different. You were a man of an entirely different sort of character than me. You *did* the kind of things the Reverend talked about, and the sort of things your son-in-law's been speaking of these last few Sundays."

He glanced over at Christopher as he said this, then back.

"You really did put other people ahead of yourself," he said, again to Pa. "You were kind, you were humble and gracious. As I said, I knew you'd do anything for me if I'd have given you the chance.

"All these years you have been a burr under my saddle, Drum Hollister. How many times I wished you'd move to Sacramento so I could be done with you! You were the constant reminder that I was not the man I should be. You were self-content, to all appearances happy and at peace with yourself and the people around you. I, on the other hand, was bitter, angry, selfish." He paused briefly, then added, "I don't mind telling you . . . I was lonely too.

"What kind of life is that! Can any man or woman be happy in such a miserable state?

"Of course not. I have money and all it can buy. I am probably the richest man for a hundred miles. But no one would mistake me for a happy man. I am nothing but a proud old selfish miser. I am getting older and grayer and richer by the day . . . but there is no happiness, no inward contentment to go along with it."

A long pause followed. Christopher said the emotion in our little bunkhouse was thicker than he'd ever experienced between three men.

"Not long ago it dawned on me," Mr. Royce went on, "that you were the man you were, free from all these miseries that hounded me. And I began to ask myself *why* you were free from them, and I began to realize it was because you had *forgiven* me. You truly treated me like a brother would treat a brother, and I knew you meant it. I tried to put you out of business. All the evil I tried to bring upon you—my God! I am mortified to admit it now!—but, Drum . . . surely you cannot have forgotten, I tried to have you killed!

"And yet . . . and yet," sighed Mr. Royce, calming and suddenly speaking very softly and shaking his head back and forth as if the very thought was still too much for him to comprehend, ". . . and yet, in spite of all that, I knew you bore me no ill will. You cast the deciding vote that kept Finchwood out of Miracle Springs back in the fifties. I knew in your heart there was nothing but love toward me.

"Ah, that knowledge burned in my soul, Drummond. It has burned in my soul till this very day. I knew I had to get it out, take the red-hot coal out of my heart and get rid of it. I knew I had somehow to make things right with you. But I didn't know how. I did not know what to do. I did not know how to replace the bitterness with forgiveness."

He stopped, drew in a breath, then glanced toward Christopher.

"Until this son-in-law of yours got up and took the pulpit the second or third week after the church made him pastor. I had already been stirred up plenty from what you told of your own history the week before that, young man," he said to Christopher. "But then on that day I'm talking about, you plunged a knife straight into me. I remember the exact words. They have burned themselves into my brain since. 'When your duty,' you said, 'becomes clear, waste not a second. Where is the first opportunity to do that thing? Go, then, and do it without delay. Then, and only then, will life spring up and blossom within you.'

"I knew my duty," Mr. Royce went on, talking again to Pa, "if I was to be a *man* and cease being this sniveling coward that I had let myself become, was to come and talk to you, Drummond. I had known it for some time, but even after young Braxton here said what he said, I couldn't bring myself to come immediately as he said. I've waited far too long. I should have done it that same week, but I just couldn't get up the courage. But then these last three nights I've hardly slept a wink, and I knew God was telling me I couldn't put it off any longer. But at last here I am—perhaps not 'without delay,' yet I am here nevertheless, prepared to do my duty, which I now see plainly enough."

He stopped and looked down at the floor. Both Pa and Christopher, Christopher told me, were bursting with love for the poor man, agonizing to see what he was having to endure at the hand of his conscience, yet unwilling to intrude in the holy moment.

"I was so aware, Corrie," Christopher said later, "of the purifying scalpel in the Father's hands, cutting through the thick crusts of self to make a door where he might himself enter and dwell with the dear man for the rest of eternity. Your father and I dared not speak. We had to allow God to carry out his own work."

After a few moments Mr. Royce looked up, then gazed straight into Pa's face and spoke again, this time in a tone of determination and resolve.

"So this is what I have come to say to you, Drummond Hollister," he said. "I want to tell you that I know now why you have the respect of your friends and the citizens of this community—it is because you are an upright and honest man. More than that, you are a good and unselfish man. You live your religion, and I want to acknowledge that to your face."

Pa nodded his gratefulness for Mr. Royce's words.

"You could have ruined me if such had been your intent," he went on. "When you helped out Douglas and Shaw when I tried to foreclose, every person in this community would have left my bank if you'd told them to. You could have opened your own bank, like you were talking about, and you'd be sitting where I am today. You could have run me out of town and everyone would have cheered.

"But you didn't. You didn't even let Finchwood bring his bank in here. I'll never forget that speech you made at the town council meeting back in '57. I'm sure you remember it?"

Pa nodded.

"Both you and Almeda voted in my favor. I had done all I could to ruin you both, and yet you sided with *me*. You talked that night about what being a Christian meant to you, and I suppose that was the first time it began to dawn on me that something was going on with you that I didn't understand. You talked about loyalty and friendship and doing good to our neighbors. I was grateful, of course, but down deep it made me even more resentful. Everyone looked up to you even more after that night. You were a bigger man than I was, and everyone knew it.

"I could never admit it, but the people chose the best man for mayor. You did good for Miracle Springs. I would only have sought good for myself. The town owes you a debt of gratitude . . . and so do I.

"So that is the second thing I want to say to you. Even though far too much time has passed since I should have said it, I'm saying it now—thank you, Hollister. I did you wrong, and you returned nothing but good to me. You were everything a friend and neighbor ought to be, though I deserved none of it.

"Then the third thing I've got to say is just this—I'm sorry for what I've done. I'm giving you my apology too for thinking wrong things about you and holding these grudges for so long.

"So I'm giving you my hand now," he said, holding out his hand toward Pa. "I know we've shaken hands before, but this time I'm giving you my hand in thanks and apology, and to say that I respect you as a man and a Christian . . . and that from now on I want to be your friend."

The two men shook hands.

Christopher said Pa's eyes had tears in them.

CHAPTER 32

PENETRATING WORDS

The two men talked a little, Pa trying to say the kinds of things that would put Mr. Royce at ease and assure him that what he'd said was true, that Pa *had* forgiven him and that there were no hard feelings whatever on his side.

"Just when I was beginning to feel downright awkward about being there with them," Christopher told me later, "Mr. Royce started talking again . . . this time to me."

"There is something else I would like to tell you—both of you," he said, "and I have you to thank for this, Mr. Braxton—"

"Please . . . Christopher," said Christopher. "If I won't let Drum call me *Reverend* I certainly cannot allow you to call me *mister*."

All three laughed, and it seemed to help Mr. Royce feel more relaxed, because Christopher said he then began to share even more freely.

"Thank you, uh . . . Christopher—that is very kind of you. I will appreciate your returning the kindness."

Christopher nodded. "But what could you possibly have to thank *me* for, Franklin?" he asked.

"For the sermons you've been preaching since becoming our pastor."

"I appreciate your encouragement. All young pastors wonder what their people are thinking."

"I can assure you that this is one member of your congregation that has been listening to every word you've said. I would like to tell you about it, if you don't mind, because it will serve as preface for a question I must ask you both."

"Of course," Christopher answered. "I am eager to hear your story."

Mr. Royce glanced over at Pa with a questioning expression.

"You bet, Franklin—go on ahead. We've got all day."

"It may just take that long," laughed the banker, a bit nervously. He wasn't too used to doing much laughing.

"I told you," he went on, again turning toward Christopher, "that your words on that one particular Sunday pierced me deeply, especially those last March about going and doing what you knew you had to do as your Christian duty.

"Everything you said penetrated so deeply. You spoke so warmly and personally about God. You spoke about living as a Christian with such force, I knew it was all the world to you and that nothing else mattered so much to you as that. You spoke about what you called Christlikeness with such longing, it was clear that to you there could be no higher goal to be attained in all the universe. And you spoke of denial and sacrifice as if they were the highest pinnacles to which a man or woman might hope to strive.

"Imagine my reaction. *Me*—be like Jesus! Franklin Royce, wealthy banker—*deny* himself . . . be a *servant*!

"The very thoughts seemed absurd.

"All my life I have subscribed to precisely those tenets you spoke of as indicating what men ordinarily believe: Get all you can . . . raise yourself up . . . possess. I have lived by the creed which says that greatness is measured by *being* served and that the *first* are first, not the last.

"Yet all the while, I considered myself a respectable 'Christian' man. I went to church and believed in God, didn't I? And while maybe I wasn't what is called as good as the next man, I was probably better than a few of them, and certainly was no murderer.

"Your words, however, brought me up short and caused me to look at myself, perhaps for the first time in my life, straight in the eye. 'If you *are* a Christian, Franklin Royce,' a little voice inside me kept saying as I sat there, 'then why is not a single one of these things the young Braxton fellow is talking about evident in your life?'

"I had never considered the first element of the kind of practical Christianity you spoke of. That I was a son of God, and that he could be a personal Father to me—never had such thoughts come within a hundred miles of my consciousness through all my years of churchgoing. That I owed obedience to him, that I ought to be poring through the Bible that sits in one of my bookcases at home—for all practical purposes like new, though I have had it for thirty years—for daily instructions about how to order my life— had someone said such things to me a year ago, I would have dismissed them out of hand. I probably would have burst out laughing at the words.

" 'This Braxton fellow *is* a radical,' another little voice said in the other side of my brain, 'by his own admission. The people in his previous church knew what they were doing when they threw him out. You may safely ignore these firebrand notions of his just as comfortably as you have ignored every other preacher you have heard.'

"But you see, Braxton—I'm sorry . . . Christopher—I *couldn't* ignore your words, for one very simple reason.

"I had been nearly knocked off my feet the week before in listening to your personal story. As I listened the second week, therefore, and in the weeks which followed, I could not ignore what you were saying, because in you I saw so much of myself. In you I saw what I might have been . . . perhaps what I *should* have been."

As Christopher heard the words, he scarcely could think what Mr. Royce might mean.

"Listening to you," the banker went on, "was like standing in front of a mirror, hearing a voice out of my own past, speaking to me about what kind of person I could have been . . . and what still might be. I was *compelled* to listen.

"I would like to tell you both why—that is, if you do not mind."

"Please," said Christopher, glancing over momentarily at Pa, "proceed."

Pa nodded his head earnestly.

CHAPTER 33

MR. ROYCE'S STORY

"Your personal story," Mr. Royce went on, "is so remarkably similar to mine that the possibility of mere coincidence seems to me impossible.

"Your father was a farmer, mine was a wealthy investment banker. Like you, I was born late in my father's life to his second wife. My mother died, like yours, when I was fourteen years old. You did not mention how much longer your own father lived. Mine died three years after my mother, and I was left alone in the world to fend for myself.

"I went from relative to relative looking for help, looking for compassion, hoping to find someone who would care whether I lived or died. But everywhere I was turned away. I too lived with aunts and uncles, all wealthy in their bank accounts but impoverished when it came to demonstrating human emotion.

"You described the feelings of worthlessness, of thinking you would never amount to anything. As you spoke I was certain no one else in that church could have known you as I did. I knew you . . . because I had been there myself. You might just as well have been describing me. Your very words struck such bitter memories in my heart.

"You spoke of your desire to go to college and to learn, and the offer your brother made you. It was a time of decision for you.

"Such a time came for me too. I was given an opportunity by one of my relatives to go to college, or I could continue in the investment firm of which my father had been a partner and hope to

161

work my way up one day into the upper echelons myself.

"In the end, I too arrived at a decision. I stood at a crossroads, just like you. But what different choices we made!

"You had suffered and been hurt, you had faced disappointment and doubts about whether you were a person worthy of life at all. You chose in the end to turn that inner grief into good. You chose to find what no human could give you, from God himself. You dedicated yourself to him and to your fellowman. You chose to help people. You chose the occupation of the ministry. You chose the road, as you put it, of serving your fellowman. Because of that decision, you are now who you are today.

"Facing the same griefs and disappointments and self-doubts, I chose a different road. I determined that I would get even with all who had turned their backs on me. I would show the world that Franklin Royce would be worth more than they ever dreamed of. I determined that I would become rich and powerful no matter who I had to hurt to achieve it. I would follow in my father's footsteps, but I would become even *more* powerful than he. Never again would anyone laugh at *me* or look down on *me*.

"Listening to you tell your tale, Christopher, made me realize so many things. I realized that, though the circumstances of every man's life vary, at the root all still face the same two basic choices— will they live for themselves as independent beings striving to *get* all they can, or, as you explained it, will they *yield* themselves to God so that they can live as his sons. It is the simple difference between trying to do good for yourself or for others . . . trying to accumulate or give away . . . trying to be first or last . . . trying to exalt yourself or your neighbor.

"You made the right choice. I see now that I made the wrong one all those years ago. It is not that one of the paths—college or investments—was right and one of them wrong. It was my *motives* which were wrong. I chose the career I did just so that I could become rich and powerful and lord it over my fellowman. I went down the road of self, and this is where it has brought me—rich . . . but empty. Do you see what I am saying? I now realize that actually—in spite of appearance—my life is one of poverty in the things that really count."

He stopped, looked away for a moment, smiled a melancholy smile, then continued.

"I learned something else, however, from my friend here," Mr. Royce added, glancing over at Pa. "From what I know of your past, Drummond, there was a time you were on the wrong road too."

"That's right, Franklin," said Pa. "For more years than I like to remember."

"That is exactly my point," Mr. Royce went on. "Because of you, I see that it is possible for a man to change roads. Even though he may have made wrong choices when he was young, perhaps many wrong choices, it is never too late. The way to that right road, the road both of you are on now, is never closed off, no matter what a man may have done."

He paused and looked seriously first at Pa, then to Christopher.

"Am I correct in making that statement," he asked, "—that it is never to late to change?"

Pa and Christopher nodded their heads together.

"You are absolutely right," answered Christopher.

"I'm the living proof, all right," said Pa. "I don't like to admit it, but I was past forty by the time I got myself over onto God's road instead of my own."

"All right then," said Mr. Royce, "we're finally to the question I came here to ask the two of you, once I got the business of my apologies to Drum out of the way. You said in your sermon, Christopher, that you were going to challenge the people of Miracle Springs, and that if we weren't comfortable being challenged to make something better of ourselves, then you weren't the man for us. Do you remember saying that?"

Christopher nodded.

"Well, I don't know about anyone else, and I cannot say I *was* comfortable with it, but I'm one man of your congregation that *does* want to make something better of myself. So I'm going to take you up on your challenge."

CHAPTER 34

A MOST WONDERFUL QUESTION

The next words out of Mr. Royce's mouth were so simple, yet so profoundly humble, that Christopher could hardly sit calmly as he listened to them.

"So I'm going to take you up on your challenge," Mr. Royce had said. "And my question is this: How *does* a man start over? How *do* you go back and undo all those years of walking down the road of self? How *do* you get onto God's road?

"You see, as strange as it sounds to be coming from my mouth, I guess the plain fact of the matter is that I've had enough of Franklin Royce. If God is a Father like you say he is . . . well, I'm ready to be his son, that is, if he'll have me, and to live like you talked about last Sunday."

I could hardly believe my ears as Christopher recounted Mr. Royce's words!

Pa looked over at Christopher in amazement. Mr. Royce looked at them both. "So," he said, "what do I do now?"

"I knew from the look on your father's face," Christopher said, "that he didn't have any idea what to say. Yet I was reluctant myself to take the lead. I felt that your father had been the primary influence in Franklin's life, even though it had been listening to what I said that finally prompted him to come and face your father and make the confession he had. I felt like your father ought to be the one to talk to him, to answer his question. It would mean more coming from someone he had known such a long time. But I knew

164

your father hadn't been in many situations like that—"

"Not a one I can think of," I said.

"That's the point. I didn't want to just get up and walk out and leave them both embarrassed and wondering what to do."

"So what *did* you do?" I asked.

"I tried to get the conversation moving in the right direction, telling him some of the same things I told Alkali Jones."

Christopher then recounted the rest of the conversation.

"Do you recall what I said last Sunday, Franklin?" Christopher said to him. "When a man or woman, a boy or girl, no matter how young or old, wants to become God's son or daughter, the process is always the same. Whether it's starting down the road for the first time or changing roads later on, as you put it . . . whether it's someone who's been going to church for years or has never set foot inside a church in his life—they all still have to do the same thing."

"That's my question," repeated Mr. Royce. "What is that thing they must do?"

"It's simply a matter of giving yourself over to your Father. Do you remember—I said that means hands, feet, brain, heart, thoughts and feelings and attitudes and behavior—everything. You're saying to him, *Here, Father . . . here is my life. I give it to you. You take charge of it now. I want you to be my Father, and I will be your good and obedient little son.* That's all there is to it."

"That's all?"

"You asked how to start over?"

Mr. Royce nodded.

"Well then, that is how to do it. That's how to make a *start*. But then you asked if that was all. And in answer to that I would say—no, it's only the beginning. Once you've done that, you've gotten onto the right road. Now you have to *walk* down that road. Now it becomes a matter of *growing*, as I also spoke of. It becomes a matter of living and behaving and thinking like the good and obedient little son you told your Father you wanted to be. So you have to find out what your Father wants you to do. It usually means unlearning many old habits and patterns and learning new ones in their place."

"How will I find out all these things?"

"He will show you. The Gospels are the beginning, as I also

explained. That's where we find out how children of the Father are to live and behave."

"What if something I need to know isn't in the Bible?"

"He will show you."

"How?"

"I cannot say. He uses different means with all of us. But if you ask for your Father's help, he will give it. Ask *him* all your questions. Ask him what *he* wants you to do. When we ask, he always answers.

"By this time," Christopher told me, "he was so broken, with all his defenses down, that he was sitting there like a little child who didn't know what to do next. It was quite wonderful.

" 'Do you want to tell the Father that you want to be his son, Franklin?' I asked.

" 'Yes . . . yes, of course I do,' he answered.

" 'Then I'm going to leave the two of you alone,' I said. Even as I said it, I saw your father look over at me with his eyes wide open. I knew he was thinking, *Don't leave me now, Christopher!* But I knew he could lead Franklin through what he needed to do just as well as I could, and that he would grow himself from the experience.

" 'Drum, would you pray with Franklin?' I said. 'Show him that there's nothing frightful about talking with our Father just as naturally as we've been sitting here talking with one another. The two of you brothers can just have a talk with your Father.'

" 'Franklin,' I said, 'I want you to know that you may come see me anytime, day or night, with any questions you may have. Once you tell the Father you want to be part of his family, that instantly makes you and me brothers, in just the same way Drum and I are brothers. We're kinfolk! And you can call on this brother of yours anytime, about anything.'

"Then I got up, left, and went over to the main house."

CHAPTER 35

LIVING EPISTLES

Christopher and I were in the house with the rest of the family when we heard Mr. Royce's buggy leave. A minute later Pa walked into the house.

The expression on his face was unlike anything I'd ever seen before. It was a dazed look—bewilderment, disbelief, and a sort of half smile all in one. He was just shaking his head, like he was trying to wake himself up, wondering if what had just gone on had actually been real.

We all watched him come in, waiting for him to say something, but he didn't seem to be able to get a single word out. He sat down in his favorite chair, still staring straight ahead and shaking his head back and forth.

"I just don't believe it," he finally said. His voice was soft, like he was speaking to himself. "You can never tell who's paying attention to what you're doing, or what folks are thinking."

We all waited again.

"I might have expected it with Alkali," he went on, his voice still soft, "—but Franklin Royce? Never would I have figured he'd have wanted anything to do with the likes of us . . . and here all the time he's looking . . . almost envious, I reckon you'd say. How can you figure a thing like that?"

Christopher had told us a little of what had gone on before Pa had returned, though there hadn't been time to tell us every detail.

"Of all people, you shouldn't be surprised, Drummond," said Almeda. "It's the very thing you spoke about in church that evening in March."

"I know," sighed Pa, still shaking his head. "But there's a difference in believing something is true and seeing it happen right before your eyes."

"What happened after I left?" Christopher now asked Pa.

"Well, we did like you said, we prayed together. It was kinda awkward there at first, couple of grown men like we were fumbling for how to say things. Praying's not exactly the sort of thing men do too much together. The last thing I ever figured I'd be doing on this earth is praying out loud with Franklin Royce!"

The rest of us smiled. We could hardly believe what God had done.

"Anyhow, I told him that praying wasn't no different than talking regular, and that you just had to think of God as right there with you. Then I kind of started out and prayed a little myself so he'd see there wasn't nothing to be afraid of. Then I stopped and told him to go on ahead and just tell God whatever was on his mind."

"Did he?" I asked Pa.

"Yeah, he did. He told God he was sorry for all the stuff he'd done and for the kind of man he'd been. He asked him to forgive him and said he hoped the people of the town would forgive him too, and asked God to help him be a better person. Then he stopped and said it again, but this time he said, '*Help me become a more Christlike person.*' "

"Hallelujah!" shouted Almeda, able to contain herself no longer. "God bless the man!"

"Then he said he wanted to be a child of God and go down God's road and be part of God's family. He asked God to help him and to show him how to be a good son. Then he stopped again and added, '*the son you want me to be.*' Then that was about it. I prayed again and said *amen* finally. We both stood up and stretched our legs, then shook hands, and he went back to town."

"That's absolutely wonderful, Drum!" said Christopher. "You did just as well as I could have done myself. It will mean more to Franklin that you were the one to pray with him."

"Praise the Lord!" added Almeda. "What wonderful things God is constantly doing in people's lives—things that we have no idea of!"

"All these years everybody thinking Franklin Royce was a skunk, and just look at what was really going on inside him," said Pa.

"I can't help but feel bad," I said. "I have to admit I have had some not-so-nice thoughts about him through the years."

"So have we all," said Almeda. "But that's over it seems. He's one of the family now!"

"I'm reminded of Paul's second letter to the Corinthians," said Christopher, "where he speaks of Christians as living epistles that people read and see what Christ can do in a human life. All these years Franklin Royce was reading each of you, especially you, Drum, all the time being drawn closer and closer to God his Father without his even knowing it."

Pa was gazing down at the floor and shaking his head back and forth again.

"You just never know who's watching, and what you might be telling them," he said, softly again. The incident had obviously gone very deep into him.

All the rest of us were quiet now too, thinking to ourselves about the people we encountered all the time without hardly giving them a second thought, wondering what they might be reading from the living epistle that was being written with each one of our lives.

CHAPTER 36

FRANKLIN ROYCE
SURPRISES THE WHOLE
TOWN

It was sometime in mid-July when the rumors started flying about Mr. Royce's bank.

At first we just began to hear about a few people who said they were renegotiating their loans. But then it started to seem like everyone we saw was talking about something to do with the bank. At first I didn't pay too much attention. But then Christopher brought it up, wondering if maybe the people of the community were experiencing some kind of financial problems. Yet we hadn't heard of anything. As far as we knew, crops this summer were growing as well as usual, and there'd been no great downturn in the price of beef or mutton. Business at the freight company seemed normal.

"I'll ask around," said Pa one evening when we were all together after supper and had gotten to talking about it.

The next day both Pa and Christopher came home with the same news, which they'd got from talking to two different people, and it explained in a second why everyone was talking: Mr. Royce had put up a notice in his bank that all *new* loans would be written for a whole percentage point lower than the existing interest rate, and that this would also apply to any *existing* loans the bank presently held for any who wanted to redraw the terms of their agreements.

Naturally everyone did!

A whole percentage point lower would make everyone's monthly payments far less than they were and would give a boost to the economy of the whole region. There was only one person, it seemed, who would possibly *not* benefit from such a change, and that was Franklin Royce himself. The next day Pa went to talk to him.

"Franklin," he said after the banker had invited him into his office and closed the door, "what's all this about the lower interest rates? Why, the whole town's talking about nothing else."

"Nothing more than it seems. I'm simply lowering my rates."

"At first I thought there was some kind of financial crisis," added Pa, "with everyone running in and out of the bank!"

Mr. Royce laughed.

"No crisis, just a normal banking procedure," he said. "Changes of interest rate aren't so unusual."

"A *lower* rate is a mite out of the ordinary!"

"Perhaps, but not unheard of."

"But a whole point—that's a huge drop. What in tarnation are you doing it for?"

"I think it's the right thing to do."

"Are the big city banks lowering their rates?"

"No," laughed Mr. Royce. "Last I heard they were up a quarter point."

"Then what if you have to borrow? It'll cost *you* more."

"Probably so."

"You've got to make a profit too."

"Don't worry, I will—albeit a somewhat slimmer one."

"We need your bank, Franklin. Where would Miracle Springs be if you go out of business?"

Again Mr. Royce laughed, delighted with Pa's concern.

"I'm not planning to go out of business anytime soon, believe me, Drum."

"Well, just tell me then what brought all this on," said Pa.

"You should know. It was something Christopher said about reading in the Gospels to find our instructions about what we're supposed to do."

"You read something like that?"

Mr. Royce nodded, but said nothing.

"Well, you gonna tell me about it?" asked Pa impatiently.

"Surely you know the story of the man called Zacchaeus?"

"I've heard the name," replied Pa.

"Well I never had," said Mr. Royce, "until I was reading a couple of weeks ago and found myself reading about him. All of a sudden I was stopped cold by the words 'and he was rich.' Suddenly something struck me I'd never thought of before—that Jesus could be the Lord of a rich man as well as a poor man."

Pa stared back at him, not realizing at first what the huge revelation was.

"I know it may not sound like much to you," Mr. Royce went on, "but I realized in that moment that I'd always thought of Christianity as more or less a religion that had more meaning the poorer you happened to be. Like I told you and Christopher, I'd gone to church for years, but I never really thought that it had much to do with *me*—after all, I was rich. I had everything I needed and more. What could God possibly do for me?"

"Reading about that Zacchaeus fellow changed your point of view, eh?" asked Pa.

"You can't imagine what the rest of that day was like for me," answered Mr. Royce. "Even after I'd talked with you and Christopher and Christopher'd said, 'You have to find out what your Father wants you to do,' I suppose I was a little skeptical. I didn't *really* think God would show *me* anything to do. I mean, I meant it when I prayed—you remember, when you and I were together, and I prayed that God would help me be a better person and know what to do. I meant it. It wasn't a phony prayer. But still, like I say, I don't know that I really expected him actually to speak to me."

"I reckon I know what you mean," said Pa. "I gotta admit I still sometimes feel that myself when I'm listening to Christopher."

"But then I remembered too," Mr. Royce said, "what Christopher said about my doing *my* part and reading in the Gospels and asking God to show me how his people are to live. So I did start reading in my Bible—for the first time, I'm ashamed to say— and I tried to look as I read for what there might be for me personally that would show me what I might be supposed to do. And then all of a sudden as I was going along in the Gospel by the man named Luke, there were those words, 'And he was rich' . . . and all at once everything changed. It was as if in an instant my whole perspective on the Bible became new—because there in its very pages was a man just like me! Do you see what I am saying, Drum?"

"I think so, Franklin," replied Pa.

"Now suddenly I could look for something to *do*—just like Christopher said—because there I was in the pages of the Book. Me—a rich man—right there talking to Jesus himself. When I had recovered my initial surprise, I read on, and the account became all the more shocking, especially when Zacchaeus said, 'I will give half of my goods to the poor, and if I have taken from anybody wrongly, I will give it back to him fourfold.' Imagine, Drum, me looking in the Gospels for something to do about my faith, and then to run across *those* words. I don't mind telling you, I could hardly sleep that night."

Pa laughed. "I reckon I'm beginning to see your problem, Franklin!"

"Over and over they repeated themselves in my brain. I had doubted whether God could speak to such a one as me . . . well, by morning I knew he *had* spoken to me. It was like nothing I'd ever experienced in my life. I had prayed a simple enough prayer . . . and here was a specific and practical answer! I'd asked to be shown something to do . . . and here was a *do* so simple and straightforward there could be no mistaking it. Here was a *do* right out of the Gospels that had to do with the very focus of my entire life—money."

Mr. Royce paused and drew in a deep breath.

"I was on my way into the bank that very next morning when something else from one of Christopher's sermons suddenly came back to me. Do you remember that day he said, 'We mustn't delay doing what we are supposed to do. Obedience postponed is disobedience.' "

"I remember," replied Pa.

"That's when I said to myself, 'Franklin Royce, it's time to see what kind of fiber you're made of, what kind of man you are. Are you going to pretend nothing happened last night? Are you going to try to talk yourself into believing God wasn't speaking to you and that all those thoughts were just nighttime fancies you can ignore now that the sun is shining and you are thinking straight again? Or are you going to *do* what you know in your heart you are supposed to do?' What it boiled down to was the question I knew I was asking myself: Are you man enough to obey?"

"Judging from what's been going on around here," said Pa with a smile, "I think I know how you answered the question."

"That very morning I put up the sign on my wall announcing that interest rates at the Royce Miners' Bank were being lowered to four-and-one-quarter percent," rejoined the banker. "It was the quickest and easiest way I could think of to return to the bank's customers anything I may have inadvertently overcharged them in the past."

"You haven't overcharged, have you, Franklin?"

"I have always tried to be fair with my interest rates," replied the banker, "but you know as well as anyone that I interpreted fair on the high side from time to time. I hope this will make up for it."

"I'm sure it will, Franklin," said Pa, "but can you afford to do so?"

"It may cause a bit of a pinch in the cash flow of the bank, but I've already been to Sacramento to secure additional funds."

"You mean to tell me you are going to have to borrow yourself in order to give back this money to the community?"

"I suppose that is the long and the short of it," said Mr. Royce, smiling.

Pa shook his head in disbelief. "Just wait till the people hear about that," he said.

"No, no, Drum, you mustn't tell them. I want no one to know why I went to Sacramento."

"But they—"

"I insist. You must promise me that word of this will not leak out. I do not want the windfall from lower interest payments and whatever else I may decide to do to be spoiled for them by sympathy for me. I would have it be a boon without any strings attached."

"What do you mean, whatever else you decide to do?" asked Pa.

"Well, there is the rest of what Zacchaeus did," replied Mr. Royce, "—giving half his possessions to the poor and restoring any wrong done four times over. I am still asking the Lord what he might want me to do in the way of those things."

CHAPTER 37

A HARD DAY IN TOWN

One day midway through the summer I put in a full day at the freight company. Actually, putting in a full day wasn't so terribly unusual. Almeda was getting so she didn't want to spend so much time in town every day and had asked me if I wouldn't mind putting in some extra hours. The business seemed to be weighing on her more than usual, and I was happy to carry more of the responsibility if I could. Christopher joined me some days as well, and we enjoyed working together.

On this particular day, however, I was the only one of the family present, and it seemed like everything that could possibly go wrong did go wrong. One of the warehouse workers came in about ten in the morning to inform me that he was quitting.

"Have you talked with Almeda?" I asked.

"I figgered you could tell her as easy as me."

"But you're going to finish out the week?" I said.

"No, ma'am—figgered on collecting what pay I got coming, and then being on my way."

"What, you mean . . . you don't mean *right now*?"

"If that'd be all right, ma'am," the man nodded. "I'd like to get what's coming to me."

"You're not even going to finish the day?" I asked, beginning to get annoyed, for the man's irresponsibility had already cost us more than he was worth.

"Didn't figger to, ma'am."

"But what about the Blackett order? Aren't you halfway through it?"

"I figgered Weber could finish it."

"Marcus is gone on deliveries all day."

"Jason . . ."

"Jason is home with his sick wife," I retorted. "I promised Mr. Blackett that order would be finished today!" By now I was thoroughly exasperated.

"I tell you, I gotta be going, ma'am. Could I get my pay?"

"You're not getting a cent from me," I said. "You come back and talk to Almeda!"

As soon as the man had gone, I turned to good, faithful Mr. Ashton, our office manager, and said, "I'm sorry you had to see that."

"Don't worry about me, Corrie. I've seen Almeda chew out a few sluggards worse than anything you ever said."

"Would you mind giving me a hand in the warehouse?" I said. "I'm afraid you and I are going to have to finish the Blackett order ourselves."

Mr. Ashton rose, placed a little sign on the door saying where we'd be, and followed me out the back door. I didn't like to ask him to help because his back wasn't the best and he was probably not even as strong as me, but we had no choice. Besides Marcus and Deal, who'd just quit, and Jason who was home with his wife, there was no one else. At the time we were a man or two thin but hadn't been able to find anyone else to hire. Now we were really shorthanded!

Sweating all over, and with my back starting to hurt, we finished up the order about noon, then hitched up a team to the wagon. I asked Mr. Ashton to drive it out to the Blackett place, explain the situation, apologize for the inconvenience, and ask Mr. Blackett if his men could unload the wagon. I went back into the office and sat down behind the desk, already tired and mentally frazzled, though the day wasn't even yet half over. I hoped Christopher might stop by to visit for a while because he was working at the McCrary place just about half a mile from town, but he didn't.

A couple of hours later, two men came in within five minutes of each other. I'd hardly seen anyone for two hours, and then there they both were in the office at the same time. Both were relative newcomers to Miracle Springs who didn't know me, didn't know Almeda, and didn't care about anything except getting their orders settled as quickly and as cheaply as possible. But both orders were complicated and it took more time and patience than either man had to see to all the details. I wished Mr. Ashton would get back!

"Look, young lady," said one of the men finally, "I've got other places to go. Can't you hurry this up?"

"I'm sorry," I said, "I'm shorthanded today and am doing the best I can."

"I never had problems like this down in Sacramento."

"Yeah, and prices are cheaper down there too," now put in the other man sarcastically.

"The price on this harness is set by the manufacturer," I said, "as is the price on that jack and the others items of *your* order," I said, turning to the second man. "We charge no more than they do in Sacramento."

"Maybe," he replied, "but they'd have everything in stock and we wouldn't have to wait for them."

I bit my tongue and didn't reply, and I did my best to finish filling out the two orders cheerfully. By the time both men left, they were still griping about our prices and delays, and I was steaming inside all over again. I wanted to shout at both of them, "Don't you know this business has been serving the people of Miracle Springs for almost twenty years and that my stepmother has given her life's blood for it?"

I went back to my work as best I could. Mr. Ashton returned, and I was glad. When Mrs. Ford came in, I let him assist her.

"Good day, Mrs. Ford," he said, rising and approaching the counter.

"Is my husband's saddle in?" she said without smiling.

"Not yet. We're expecting it any day."

"He told me not to take no for an answer."

"I'm sorry, there's nothing we can do to hurry it up. It's already on its way. I believe I told him it would be a week, and that was five days ago."

"He said it should have been in by now."

"As I said, it could be any day. We'll deliver it to your husband the moment it arrives."

She turned and left in a huff, muttering something about the service not being what it once was and closing the door with an extra hard yank of her hand.

By the end of the day I was worn out emotionally and physically. I could see why occasionally Almeda needed a break!

I rode home, still not having seen Christopher since morning. As I walked into our little bunkhouse I was looking forward to a quiet cozy evening with him. I noticed how cold and dark it was inside, having had no people there all day. The air felt like it had stopped moving, and the very stillness was heavy.

I went to work quickly to make it feel like a home again. I built a fire in the stove and began stirring up a batch of muffins. I still had some stew left over from the day before. Most of all, I just wanted some time with Christopher to share my frustrations from the day.

As the house began to warm up I began to recover from my fatigue, looking forward all the more to sitting down with Christopher and enjoying our quiet and peaceful evening together.

I had the table set and the food all ready by the time Christopher came home. He was later than I expected, and I had begun to wonder what was keeping him. I went outside a time or two, looking up the road toward town and listening for the sound of his horse. I picked a few sprigs of lavender I had planted out of the yard, and with a few forget-me-nots made a pretty little bouquet.

I walked back inside and put the flowers in a vase and set it on the center of the table. Just as I was finishing with it, I heard a horse approach. I went out just as Christopher dismounted. He came toward me, smiled weakly, and kissed the top of my forehead as he handed me his lunch can.

"Welcome home!" I said. "A hard day?"

"Yeah, and I'm pretty dirty too," he nodded. "I think I'll go out back and chop up some kindling."

"Don't you want to get cleaned up?"

"Not just yet. And I've got to put the horse away." He turned to go.

"But supper's all ready and waiting."

"You go ahead. I'm not very hungry."

With that he turned and went back to his horse and slowly led him toward the barn. I stood watching, wondering what was the matter. I sighed and walked back into the bunkhouse. I took out what he hadn't eaten from his lunch can, wondering why he hadn't finished the slabs of buttered bread and the apple. I rinsed the can out. A few minutes later I heard the sound of the ax begin chopping away out back.

Finally I couldn't stand it anymore. I went outside and slowly approached. Christopher was chopping away as if it were morning rather than the end of a long day.

"What's wrong?" I asked as he finished one piece of wood and reached down for another.

He glanced up, seemingly surprised at the sound of my voice, with an expression almost as if he'd forgotten I existed. "Oh, nothing," he said.

I stood there just a moment longer, then turned and went back inside, unable to prevent myself starting to get mad. I thought we were supposed to talk and share with each other!

I dished out some stew, buttered a muffin, and sat down at my place at the table and tried to eat. But I could only swallow one spoonful. It tasted terrible! Then I started to cry. What was going on?

Finally I got up and went across the room and sat down with a quilt on the little sofa, where I cried myself to sleep.

I woke up with Christopher shaking me and telling me it was time to go to bed. It was dark outside and obviously late. I didn't know what had happened to the dinner, but the chill told me the fire was out. I got up sleepily and we both silently prepared ourselves for bed. My heart ached.

When I woke up the next morning Christopher was already gone. When I saw him again the following evening, his spirits were better, though I never did find out what had been bothering him.

CHAPTER 38

LEARNING TO BE A PASTOR'S WIFE

Christopher had told me earlier that I didn't need to do or learn anything particular in the way of being a pastor's wife and that it would happen naturally. At the time I hadn't really understood *what* it was that would happen.

Now I was beginning to find out!

It was just involvement with people every day. That was enough to keep me growing, and not always in pleasant ways. That involvement with people wore on Christopher and led to unforeseen burdens and sometimes silences that weren't always pleasant, as happened after that long frustrating day I had worked at the freight company. But even when our times with other people were on the pleasant and enjoyable side, it was just taxing suddenly to have so little time alone for ourselves. That was the hardest part—the demands of time.

"One of the main things, Corrie," Christopher had told me earlier, "is simple hospitality. The pastor's home, even if it is just a bunkhouse, has to always be open to people. But that won't be hard for you, because you enjoy having people over anyway. Why, the Hollister place has had people coming and going ever since I came here!"

I figured I could do that well enough. It was fun to have people over to our place and to fix a nice dinner or serve coffee and cake and to sit and talk and pray with them as Christopher's wife and helper and partner.

But I also began to learn that there was more to hospitality than I might have thought at first. It was also a kind of warm hominess pointed in a different direction than toward the people of the community—toward Christopher himself.

Sometimes Christopher came home positively excited about the work he had been doing or some conversation he had had, and he would proceed to tell me all about it. That's how it was after the talk with Mr. Henry about the anger rock.

But then there were other times when he would be real silent all evening, like when he'd gone out to chop wood. I couldn't help but think he was upset with me, maybe about the way the supper tasted or how the house looked. My mind would start racing, and I'd listen to all the talk we'd had that morning over again to myself, wondering what I might have said or done to make him get so quiet.

Sometimes I'd get up the courage to ask if something was wrong, and he'd look at me with a funny expression, then sort of half smile and shake his head and answer no. Sometimes he'd sigh and start to tell me about some poor man or woman he'd met up with that day and how he'd been praying for him ever since.

It was always difficult for me, because I was so prone to take things on myself and think that something was my own fault when Christopher wasn't talkative. But gradually I realized that there were emotional demands to pastoring that were even harder to bear sometimes than the physical demands of hard work.

I began to see that hospitality meant more than just having folks over. It meant providing a safe and peaceful and restful place for Christopher, where he could talk with me when he wanted, but also where he could be free not to talk too. Sometimes he just needed to be quiet to think and pray or reflect on what might have happened during the day—or even to go out and chop wood and ignore me if he needed to, without my getting upset about it. He needed our home to be a sanctuary and a retreat for *his* soul, just as much as other people might have needed it to be a friendly place to visit when they needed to talk about something.

Even as I write that, it sounds easier than it was. It *wasn't* easy to learn. And I didn't just learn it all of a sudden. I continued to struggle to learn it, and I am *still* having to learn new aspects of it every day. That was *really* a hard day when I cried myself to sleep. But I tried to learn from the experience.

Our lives weren't just our own anymore. We belonged to the whole community. There was a certain sacrifice that went along with it, of both time and emotional energy. Not only did I need to be gracious to people when they came to visit, I needed to allow Christopher the freedom to continue thinking and praying for them or even carrying a burden on their behalf after he came home, without trying to claim all his energy and attention for myself.

As I said, that was not easy. All I'd had to worry about before was myself. I could read or write or take off on horseback anytime I wanted to. Being married had, of course, changed that. And now being a pastor's wife had changed it all the more. There wasn't the same freedom as before. Now I had to be there when Christopher needed me. Being hospitable meant putting others ahead of myself, most of all my husband and the ministry God had led him into.

They say you don't really learn to appreciate what your parents did for you until you have children of your own. I suppose your eyes are not fully opened to anything until you have looked upon it with the eyes of your own personal experience. In the same way, I'm sure you cannot really see what being a wife is all about until you *are* one.

Now I was one. And now I began to see that a lot of what Almeda did for Pa and Aunt Katie did for Uncle Nick, and what Harriet had done for Rev. Rutledge, was practicing hospitality toward their men as well as toward their families and visitors, making their homes a place where they could regain their strength to go back out to do what God had given them to do.

But I struggled to learn it almost every day, it seemed! When Christopher came home after my difficult day at the freight company, I'd tried to be hospitable with the supper and the flowers, but in my heart I got angry, which was anything but hospitable. As I said, it was a daily learning experience!

Late one other afternoon a week or two later, I was fixing supper and feeling frustrated because I had been trying to find time all day to squeeze in an hour or so to write in my journal about these new things I was trying to learn. But almost from the moment I'd climbed out of bed, the day had just been too full with unexpected interruptions. Christopher was working across the valley helping one of the ranchers brand some new cattle, and I hadn't seen him since seven that morning. I'd worked some at the freight company that morning, then Harriet had come over for lunch. Ruth was sick, and I'd helped Almeda for a while with her.

Then of all things, about three in the afternoon Mrs. Gilly and Mrs. Sinclair came to visit. When I looked out the window and saw them driving up in Mrs. Sinclair's buggy I couldn't help groaning. Oh, how I hoped they had come to see Almeda! But no, they got out and headed straight for our bunkhouse.

With a sigh, I went over to stoke the fire in the stove and put on the teapot. By the time I heard the knock on the door I had managed to find a smile, though my heart was not in the mood for the hour-and-a-half visit which followed.

I was so worn out by the time they left, from having to keep a smile plastered on my face and keep up my end of a positively uninteresting conversation about ninety minutes of nothing, with the feeling all the while that they were both looking for any tidbit of gossip they might pounce upon and proceed to spread throughout Miracle Springs. They would probably have been gone after twenty minutes if I'd intentionally let slip some little personal morsel about Christopher or me!

And now there I sat peeling potatoes when I really wanted to be writing, or outside on a walk, or someplace other than right there. I hadn't had a minute to myself all day.

Finally I just decided I was going to *take* the time.

I threw down my knife, wiped my hands on my apron, and walked to the tiny writing desk. If supper was a little late tonight, well that would be too bad. I flipped through my journal to the first clean page. The last entry had been almost a week ago. I couldn't believe it! I used to write pages and pages every day. Now I was lucky to get to my journal once a week!

I filled my pen with ink, and on the top of the page I wrote the words, *Hospitality and the Pastor's Wife.*

Then I sat staring at what I had written. My brain was blank.

I sat for five or ten minutes. Nothing would come.

Suddenly behind me I heard the door open. I jumped up quickly, for some reason embarrassed at the thought that Christopher would find me sitting at the desk.

"Hey, Corrie!" he said, walking toward me and kissing me as I turned around. "What are you working on?"

"Oh . . . oh, nothing—but you're a mess!" I exclaimed, trying to change the subject. He really was. His face was grimy and his clothes were covered with dust.

"It was filthy work, and I'm exhausted."

"You're home earlier than I expected."

"I'd have never lasted another hour. Luckily we got done."

He started to take off his overgarments and toss them in the corner.

"I'm going to go take a bath in the creek. What's for supper?"

"Uh . . . potatoes and biscuits," I said.

"Good, I'm starved."

As soon as he was gone I hurried back to finish the potatoes and get them into the pot and boiling. It wasn't long before I realized how ridiculous I'd been—trying to write about hospitality when inside I was being just as inhospitable as could be, both to my visitors and my husband, and fooling myself into thinking I had anything worthwhile to say on the matter. *I guess hospitality isn't something you can write about—you have to do it!* I said to myself.

By the time Christopher was back from the creek and into a fresh set of clothes, supper was almost ready. But I'd forgotten to close my journal, and he glanced down as he passed at the empty page with the ambitious heading.

"What's this?" he said as he paused next to my desk. "Looks like you were getting ready to write something I would be interested to read."

"I doubt that," I laughed.

"Why?"

"Good idea . . . bad timing," I said. "I don't think I'm quite ready to write about being a pastor's wife, even in my journal!"

CHAPTER 39

THE FREIGHT COMPANY

Almeda turned fifty that summer. Pa was now fifty-three. I know the passage of years can't help but bring changes, yet when you're young you don't stop to think about things with quite the same perspective as you do when you get older. So I think it came as a surprise to us "younger adults" one evening when Pa and Almeda asked us to all have supper together because they had something they wanted to talk to us about.

"Almeda and I aren't getting any younger," began Pa, and I could tell from his expression that something serious was on his mind. "And we've been thinking and talking and praying about the future and about some changes we maybe ought to make."

We all glanced around at each other, wondering what he might be talking about.

"The long and the short of it," Pa went on, "is that we've been talking about selling the freight company."

He stopped to let his words sink in. I don't know what anyone else thought. But the Mine and Freight—now officially the Hollister Supply Company—had been such a part of our lives since the very day my brothers and sisters and I had first set foot in Miracle Springs that I could hardly imagine our lives going on without it.

"The business continues to grow," now added Almeda, "and we are simply beginning to feel that it is too much for us. It seems as though the business needs new, young, fresh energy. Mr. Parrish and I had that kind of enthusiasm when we first began back during the gold rush. But times have changed. The demands on the business are different now. We've done our best to change with them, and yet at the same time we're not at the stage of life when we have the energy or vision to begin all over again in new directions."

"What new directions?" asked Tad.

"Nothing particular, son," replied Pa. "We've just got the feeling that new times are coming. Why, the railroad's going to link the country within a year. That's bound to change a lot of things. More folks'll be coming west. More lines are getting built right here in California. A business like ours that has to do with transporting things is bound to change by all that modernizing."

"We want to see the business continue to thrive," said Almeda, "but we're wondering if it might be able to do so better in someone *else's* hands. You know—young, fresh, enthusiastic blood."

"But you *are* the freight company," I protested.

"Yes, dear," admitted Almeda, "I have been. But perhaps that season is drawing to a close, as sad as it makes me to say it."

It fell silent around the table.

"'Course any of you'd have first crack at the business and would be our first choice to carry on with it," said Pa after a minute. "That's why we're talking it over like this, to ask you all what you think, and to see if any of you'd ever thought of taking a more permanent interest in things."

Again it was quiet a moment.

"What would *you* do, Pa?" asked Zack.

"Maybe become your deputy!"

"No you won't, Drummond Hollister!" exclaimed Almeda. "If we're talking about being too old to keep running the freight company, then . . . well, I won't finish what I was going to say!"

Pa laughed. "I don't know, son," he said to Zack. "There's plenty around here to keep me busy. Maybe I'll do what most men my age do and raise a few cattle and horses to sell. We're all right for money, especially if we sell the business. I'll keep as busy as I want to with the mine—there's still some gold there."

"What about politics again, Pa?" I asked.

"Not for me, Corrie. Even with the train coming through here, I've got no intention of running back and forth to Sacramento again. The one thing I aim to do is enjoy my later years with my family. I'm staying put right here in Miracle Springs!"

"We had thought at one time about you and Corrie taking over the business," said Almeda, now turning toward Christopher. "But of course now that would seem out of the question."

"Why?" I asked. "If we're not going to take money from the church, then we have to support ourselves somehow. Besides, I know more about the freight company than anyone but you—well, maybe you or Mr. Ashton."

"The question is, Corrie," replied Almeda, "—do you really *want* to run a business yourself?"

"There's more to it than meets the eye," said Pa. "Even as close to it as you have been, you don't realize a tenth the burden it's been for Almeda all these years. You just don't feel it till you're standing in those shoes yourself."

"Your father's right, Corrie," said Almeda. "I have no doubt you and Christopher could do a most capable job of it. But is it what the Lord wants for you? A business can be a huge emotional burden, just like a church."

"I imagine there are more similarities between the two than most people realize," said Christopher, "and they take their toll."

"There are always pressing financial problems," Pa put in, "situations with employees, disgruntled customers, orders that are late, competition, and a thousand complexities. I can't tell you how many times Almeda's come home plumb worn out from them."

"It is exciting and challenging if that is what you make the focus of your whole life. I have loved being in business all these years," said Almeda. "But your father is right, there are burdens it brings. And when you have other responsibilities—as the two of you now do with the church and all its needs—then it becomes very difficult to have enough of you to go around."

"I see," nodded Christopher. "These are all things we must seriously consider."

"The years, for example, when your father was in the legislature," added Almeda, "—those were difficult years for us to keep up the energy necessary in the business, along with all the demands of his political role."

"Not to mention the fact," laughed Christopher, "that I know nothing about business."

"Neither did I, son," added Pa. "But these women of ours are mighty capable. I have no doubt Corrie could run the business just as good as Almeda did—*if* that's what was the right thing."

"And that's really the point, isn't it," said Christopher, "—what is the *right* thing? What does God want? Corrie and I will pray earnestly about it," he said, turning first to Pa, then to Almeda.

I nodded my agreement.

"And, of course, we've thought of the rest of you too," Pa said now to the others. "Zack, you're pretty tied up with what you're doing. Tad, I don't know what you're planning on doing, but—"

"I'm going to sea, Pa."

Pa laughed. "I know I've heard you talk about sailing from time to time, and I see you reading them books about ships—you really serious, son?"

"You bet I am, Pa. I'm gonna do it someday."

"And after that, what?"

"Don't know. Haven't thought much about it."

"Becky?"

"I don't know, Pa," Becky replied.

Again there was a long, thoughtful silence.

"What about Mr. Ashton?" asked Zack.

"We shall perhaps talk to him," answered Almeda, "but I am not certain he would be best for the future of the business, either. He is even older than we are."

"Well, we ain't likely to settle anything here and now," said Pa. "We just wanted to know what you all thought. Meantime, we're gonna write to Mike and Emily and let them know what we're thinking. We'll keep praying, and all you keep praying, and we'll see what the Lord wants to do."

CHAPTER 40

LOOKING TOWARD THE FUTURE

Along with everything else, 1868 was a presidential year.

Andrew Johnson had become President after President Lincoln's assassination in 1865. He did his best to carry out Mr. Lincoln's reconstruction policies, which were already in place. However, he was not as strong a leader as Mr. Lincoln and was not able to carry them out very well.

Mr. Lincoln's plan had been to view the southern states as never having been outside the Union. So immediately after the war they had been fully recognized as states just like always, and President Johnson had laid down conditions for the restoration of their state governments. New constitutions, legislatures, and governors had been established in these states, and their first act had been to ratify the Thirteenth Amendment of the Constitution, which abolished slavery.

The Congress, however, controlled by Northerners, did not approve of President Johnson restoring the South so quickly by presidential authority. Congress wanted to keep treating the southern states as rebel territories and to withhold the full rights of statehood. Had President Lincoln lived, this battle for power between the President and Congress might have turned out differently. But with Mr. Johnson being a weak leader, Congress slowly gained the upper hand and proceeded to ignore his proclamations and pass its own series of reconstruction acts. Mr. Lincoln's more moderate and forgiving approach to putting the country back together after the war was thus replaced by a harsher and more arrogant Congressional scheme led by the radical Republicans of the President's own party.

The dispute between Congress and the President became so severe that finally Congress decided to try to get rid of President Johnson by impeachment.

In May of that year two things happened. President Johnson was narrowly acquitted in the impeachment proceedings, which meant that he would not be removed from office. Yet his reputation was so low that he was not nominated to run again on the Republican ticket. Instead, that same month, at their national convention in Chicago, the Republicans nominated Ulysses S. Grant as their presidential candidate for the election to be held that November.

If anything could have tempted me to get involved again in politics, that could have!

Knowing Mr. Grant personally as I felt I did, it would have been easy to start writing articles supporting him, maybe even speaking as I had for President Lincoln's and Mr. Stanford's campaigns. So much rushed back to my mind as I read the newspaper accounts throughout that summer—from Mr. Grant's first visit right here to Miracle Springs way back in 1853 to my associations with him during the war.

Suddenly I had three possible things to be involved in—being the wife of a pastor, running a business, and politics and newspaper writing.

But now there was a lot more for me to think about than just myself. I had a husband to consider, and we had a church and a community that was looking to us to be there for them when they needed us. So Christopher and I had been praying diligently about all these things.

Besides, I wasn't sure I wanted to be in politics anymore. Meeting Christopher, and of course being married, had gradually changed everything. So much of what had once been important no longer looked the same in my eyes.

Almeda had given me wise counsel that night when we were talking about the future of the freight company. As time passed, I did not find rising up within myself a strong desire or enthusiasm toward either the business *or* politics.

Both still interested me. But I was slowly recognizing that Christopher's and my future lay in other directions. I recognized too that this lessening of enthusiasm in one direction, with increased focus in another, was the Lord's subtle and quiet way of answering our prayers about whether we were to be involved in the future of the freight company in a more permanent way.

CHAPTER 41

WHAT IS GOING TO LAST?

Throughout the summer and early fall Christopher and I continued to talk about the future and where these different things fit into our new roles in the community now that Rev. Rutledge was gone. One day we were talking about my writing again in a casual way, and this led into a discussion about permanency. Christopher would have been happy for me to keep writing, for he had always supported it wholeheartedly, yet he always led me back to consider the other side of it too.

"We've always got to look at the long-term impact of what we do," Christopher said as we were talking.

"How do you mean?" I asked. "My writing something that's going to be of interest years from now rather than just for the present?"

"Something like that, I suppose," he replied. "But it's not just writing. I try to consider the lasting quality of what I do as a pastor too."

"Isn't everything you do as a pastor lasting?" I asked.

"I'm not sure you can say that. I think even a pastor can get caught up in temporal and insignificant things like anyone else."

He paused thoughtfully.

"It's something I started thinking about during those long years at Mrs. Timms' farm," he went on after a moment. "What's going to last?—that's always got to be the question one asks. What's going to outlive us, what are we going to do in life that lives beyond us, what efforts of ours now will we still be able to look back from eternity and see the results of?"

"What kinds of things do you mean?"

Christopher laughed.

"That is the very question I've been asking myself all these years. I suppose it began when I was asked to leave my first church. As I looked back on my ministry among those people, and all the sermons I preached and all the other pastoral functions I carried out, I could not help but wonder if they would all go up in the first puff of smoke with all the rest of the wood, hay, and stubble that Paul talks about."

"That seems a rather harsh judgment," I said. "Surely you did *some* good?"

Christopher smiled. "I suppose so. And yes, I remember individuals here and there that I like to think I helped in some ways that will be permanent. But do you see the question I'm trying to raise—that what looks on the surface to be a good, even a spiritual thing—like the preaching of sermons, for instance, which I did lots of—or even just a good thing by itself—like writing articles helping people to see political issues more clearly—may or may *not* have any eternal value?"

"How can you know?"

"That's the hard part! I've got no easy answer. I only know that I want to spend my energies on things that do have eternal value. But I still have to look hard to know what they are sometimes. One thing I have been in the habit of doing whenever something comes along that I have to decide about is to ask myself, if I were eighty or ninety years old and facing near death, looking back on my life, would this be something I was glad I devoted time and energy to. That is one of the things I asked myself in arriving at a decision regarding the offer from the church last March. It's amazing how quickly that simple question sifts the wheat from the chaff."

"What makes the difference between the two, the wheat and the chaff?"

Christopher thought for a moment.

"I suppose the things that have eternal value have to do with character, with the kind of people we *are* more than the things we do. *Internal* things rather than external. It's not always as easy as saying that we ought to be helping people. If we're not becoming more Christlike as a result, then of what permanent value is it? I may fix a broken buggy for widow Hutchins like I did last week, but if inside I am annoyed about the inconvenience, what will be the permanent benefit to my eternal character from having done it?"

"What about Mrs. Hutchins?" I asked. "She benefits whether you were annoyed or not."

"Benefits . . . how? By having her wagon in good working order? How does that benefit *her* eternally? That wagon will go up with all the rest of the wood, hay, and stubble."

"Hmm . . . I see what you mean," I said.

I thought for a moment more. Then I had another thought.

"But what if your fixing her buggy benefited Mrs. Hutchins *internally*?" I said. "What if you helped *her* eternal character somehow by doing it?"

"Exactly!" rejoined Christopher. "I think you've hit it precisely. When *we* are becoming more internally Christlike from what we do, or when we are in some small way helping *another* man or woman to become more internally Christlike themselves . . . then it seems to me that we are expending our energies upon things of eternal value."

"How wonderful," I added, "if both can be happening at once."

"Amen to that!" said Christopher. "The more I think and pray about this, I just can see nothing else but Christlikeness of character that is going to last. Everything else we do, everything else we are, is going to vanish the instant we die. Some poor individuals will be left with very impoverished natures. Others will find themselves giants of character in the kingdom of heaven because of the multitude of small acts and choices of Christlike kindness they demonstrated in this life. Turning ourselves constantly toward such a focus, and helping others to orient their lives likewise toward Jesus, seems to be life's ultimate goal. That's what I want our ministry in Miracle Springs to be."

"But not everyone can be a preacher like you."

"I don't mean *telling* people about Christlikeness. No, I don't necessarily mean *talking* about spiritual things at all. I mean behaving in such a way that Christlikeness of character results—both in yourself and in others. Acting, thinking, speaking, responding . . . living as much as possible like Jesus did and according to what he taught—it cannot help but have eternal consequences. No, I don't mean preaching about it, but modeling our lives after his."

"Like Pa and Mr. Royce."

"Precisely. Your father hadn't the slightest idea what was happening. But because he was behaving and thinking in more Christlike ways himself—forgiving, being kind to others, turning the other cheek—Mr. Royce was all the while being drawn toward Christlikeness himself. Therefore, both men are now engaged in the development of internal characters that will go with them into eternity."

"Speaking of Mr. Royce, what he has been doing still has everyone in the whole town abuzz. Did I tell you that Almeda received a letter just yesterday from her friend in Sacramento, Carl Denver?"

Christopher shook his head with a puzzled expression.

"No, what about?"

"There are banking people in Sacramento that have had their eye on expanding up here for years," I said. "They'd heard about Mr. Royce's lowering the interest rate on all his loans, just at the time all the Sacramento banks were raising theirs. He asked Almeda if Royce's bank was in trouble."

Christopher smiled.

"Almeda laughed when she read it," I said. " 'Just wait until I write and tell him that Franklin has also canceled one month's payment on all loans so that his valued customers may catch up on their other bills,' Almeda said. 'He'll think the good banker of Miracle Springs has gone completely mad!' "

Christopher nodded, still smiling, but almost reverently. What Mr. Royce had done was to him a serious and holy thing.

"The Zacchaeus principle," he said after a moment. "I was so moved when I heard what he had done. It showed that what happened between him and your father, and the prayers he prayed, were going to be permanent and were going to make a lasting difference in his life. Following up prayers of Christlikeness with actions of sacrifice and kindness gives the Father a tremendous foothold from which to work rapid transformations of character. God bless the man."

"It seems he already is."

"I truly believe Franklin Royce is going to be a radiant son of his new Father."

We thought a few moments. It was still hard to believe what a change had come over Mr. Royce so quickly.

"This is an example of exactly what we were talking about," Christopher began after a minute. "Your father, as he represents it in talks we've had, saw in your mother and then Almeda and Avery Rutledge qualities of character that eventually prompted him to want to live in a different way himself. His life, in turn, as that same Christlike character began to emerge, has shown something to Franklin Royce about how he wants to live and the kind of person he wants to be. Now Franklin in his turn is beginning to demonstrate an unselfishness and a Christlike spirit of giving that I know will have profound impact within others of this community, perhaps even so far away as Sacramento."

"Wow, that is a wonderful progression!"

"Christlikeness always multiplies. It cannot but have deep and lasting impact on all those it touches.

"That's the eternal value we've been talking about. When your father dies, it won't be his work at the mine or the gold he's dug up or the votes and speeches he made in Sacramento that will go with him into the next life, but rather the Christlikeness of character he's developed in the process of these other pursuits. And I think the rewards Paul speaks of that he will receive there will be made up of the Christlikeness of character he has helped to foster in others, such as Franklin Royce."

I nodded.

"Anyway, that's how I view it now," said Christopher, "though it's a complex mystery. I only pray our lives can be influential in the same eternal way as your father's has."

CHAPTER 42

A PERMANENT LEGACY

"What does all this have to do with my writing?" I asked after we had again sat thinking silently for a few minutes. "Does looking at the lasting and eternal importance of everything mean I should only write about spiritual things? I doubt Mr. Kemble would be very excited about that."

Christopher laughed lightly.

"I'm not sure *that's* what it means, and that wasn't what I was trying to say. You know me well enough by now to recognize that the term *spiritual* for me encompasses all of life, not just things connected with church services, hymns, and Bible verses."

"What did you mean I should do then?"

"You'll have to pray and ask the Lord to answer that question more clearly than I can."

"I want to know what you think anyway."

"Well then . . ." began Christopher, then paused, pursing his lips and scratching his neck as he thought about it. "Maybe I would say this—that God is probably able to use any kind of writing, just like he is able to use any other kind of thing people do—whether it be preaching, working a gold mine, or running a bank—to draw men and women closer to him. I don't know that it's so much what you write about exactly, but that the process helps *you* in the development of *your* Christlike character and enables you to help *others* toward that same end."

I reflected on what Christopher had said for a moment.

"But," I said at length, thinking out loud, "writing is different than everything else. Your readers don't actually see you living your life in a daily way like Mr. Royce was able to see Pa all these years. So how could I possibly have an impact in people's lives toward Christlikeness unless somehow I wrote about it more directly?"

"Hmm . . . I see what you mean."

"What possible difference could it make whether somebody votes for so-and-so—after we get to heaven?" I asked. "I hope Mr. Grant wins the election. But how can that be a so-called spiritual thing? What eternal difference does it really make?"

"In other words, what could be more temporal and passing than politics?"

"Maybe that's what I'm asking, and if that is true, why should I expend energy and time writing about it? How does that help people toward developing Christlike characters?"

I stopped, and kind of half shook and half nodded my head with indecision.

"And yet . . ." I went on, "I *love* to write. I admit it. I don't think I could ever *not* write."

"Then by all means keep writing!" said Christopher. "I would never want you to stop."

"But about what? Most of what I've written articles about in the past isn't of much eternal significance."

"Writing doesn't have to be published to have value. Maybe you'll write articles in the future, maybe you won't. But you should keep writing regardless. Maybe your audience won't be newspaper readers at all. What about the journals we both keep?"

"I don't write in mine much anymore, it seems," I laughed. "Remember my hospitality entry!"

"How's it going?"

"The page is still empty, but I'm going to go back and fill it pretty soon!"

"But however much or little time we find for such writing, it is still important, even though mostly it's just for ourselves and our thoughts when we're alone with God."

"I suppose you're right."

"And with the other writing you do—we don't always know who our audience is going to be when God is writing the living

200

epistles of our lives. Your father didn't know Mr. Royce was 'reading' him. I simply think if you write—write whatever the Lord gives you to write—he will make use of it in his own way."

I nodded.

"Would you like to know a different kind of writing I've been doing in my own journal over the last year or so?" Christopher went on.

"Yes . . . of course," I answered.

"Actually it began after I'd come here and had begun to think of marriage in a more personal way than I ever had before. I never said anything to you about it, however, because it seemed somehow premature to talk about us having a family before we were married. And then it's never come up since the wedding."

"Go on, then, tell me," I urged.

"I've found myself thinking, again as if I were an old man like I sometimes do, of what I would want to say to my sons and daughters—*our* children, I mean!—if I knew I was about to leave them. What would be the spiritual principles I would want to pass on to them—almost like a legacy?"

"Oh, Christopher, it's almost too much to imagine our really having children someday."

"I certainly hope we do. Don't you?"

"Of course. But doesn't the thought seem, I don't know, frightening?"

"How so?"

"I never anticipated being a wife—but being a *mother*, now that seems even more of an awesome responsibility! Although what woman isn't eager for it at the same time. But go on with what you were saying."

"Well, sometimes thinking of being a father helps me pray and focus on what the truly important things in life are now. It has helped *me*, even if no one else ever does read it."

"Oh, I *want* to read it . . . that is, if you would let me."

"You will. But I was only telling you to suggest that you could do the same in your journal. You have learned so many things over the years as you have been growing with the Lord. Do you remember what you told me you were going to do with the journal I gave you back in Virginia?"

"Of course. I said I was going to write down very special thoughts and ideas and spiritual truths that were important and that I didn't ever want to forget."

"Have you begun?"

"I've done some of it."

"Well, that's the kind of thing I mean. That's what I'm doing in my journal too. Just imagine what a heritage these will be to pass on to our own sons and daughters someday."

"Oh, it *would* be. I see what you're saying! Sometimes I so long to know what Ma was like—I mean really like down inside. I want to know what she thought about spiritual things, how she talked and listened to the Lord. I was so young then that I wasn't able to see that part of her. Now that I am an adult myself, married, and the same age as Ma was when I have memories of her, sometimes I hunger so much to know more of what *she* thought and felt."

"I think all children long to know their parents better, especially, as you say, when they reach maturity themselves. I share that feeling so intensely, mostly for my mother because she died when I was young, but even for my father in a way too, even though I was afraid of him. I even find places of fondness occasionally springing up within me toward his memory, realizing how little he understood the role of fatherhood with which God had entrusted him. Now that I think about being a father myself, I find my feelings toward him much more tender than when I was younger."

"I feel it more for Ma too," I said. "Maybe it's because she's gone, or because I'm her daughter. Though even as wonderful as Pa is, sometimes he can be so exasperatingly tight-lipped. I long to know what *he* thinks and feels too."

"One of the great problems we men have," laughed Christopher.

"That's one of the things I love so much about you, Christopher! How can I have been so lucky as to get a man who talks and communicates!"

"Just think what a treasure it would be if we had in our possession letters, thoughts, journals of our mothers," he went on, not to be sidetracked by my outburst.

"It would be priceless!"

"Especially their spiritual ideas, their struggles, their walks with the Lord, what they placed values on, what their priorities in life were, what principles they tried to live by. What a wonderful gift to be afforded such a glimpse into our parents' hearts."

I sighed. As exciting as the thought was, how could I not be saddened at the same time by the realization that I never would know my mother as well as I might wish I could—not in this life, at least.

"That's why I've begun writing down those kinds of things," Christopher said quietly, sensing my mood. "If the Lord honors me by allowing me to be a father one day, perhaps a grandfather many years from now, I want to have just such a treasure to pass on to our sons and daughters, and their sons and daughters after them—to all our descendants perhaps even into the next century— of the things that this husband and wife—you and me, Corrie— valued in our lives with God our Father."

I sat thinking for a moment about what Christopher had said. Then another thought occurred to me and I smiled.

"What are you thinking?" he asked.

"About something you said in your first sermon at the church," I answered.

Christopher arched his eyebrows in question, waiting for me to go on.

"Do you remember when you said that if they made you their pastor, you would constantly challenge the people of Miracle Springs?"

"I remember."

"I find your words now a great challenge to *me*."

"How so?"

"To think of my writing as something longer lasting than newspaper articles and political elections, or even books . . . to look beyond writing to be published to the writing of spiritual truths that can be passed on to future generations—our own children and grandchildren, and who knows who else."

"I guess that is something like what I have been thinking, though I wasn't consciously trying to issue a challenge."

"What an opportunity—to actually be able to frame a legacy to leave to those that come after you, about the times you've lived in, and mostly about what truths the Lord showed you about life and the world, about people, about yourself, and about him."

"That is exactly what the Lord has been impressing upon me. And since we both enjoy expressing ourselves with the pen, it seems we ought to be attentive to his leading."

"And write, you mean?"

"Yes. I'm certain the Lord will continue to use your writings to help people know him better, Corrie, though henceforth it may be in new ways different from what he has done in the past. I hope he might even be able to find something to use in what I am compiling too."

"He will—I'm sure of it, Christopher. And as long as you're part of it with me," I said, "I will look forward to whatever changes the future brings with anticipation and eagerness."

CHAPTER 43

A DOUBLE TITHE

When Franklin Royce came to call again, it was one afternoon when Christopher happened to be alone at the church. The banker walked over from town rather than riding his buggy. He wanted no one to know that he and Christopher were having a private conversation, for reasons which Christopher only told me about much later.

"You know your family tithe fund that's in my bank?" Mr. Royce began once they were seated.

"The *church's* fund," said Christopher.

"Yes . . . right. A tithe is ten percent, is it not?"

"That's correct, Franklin."

"Well," Mr. Royce went on, "I've been thinking more about what we talked about before . . . you remember, about Zacchaeus and returning fourfold, and all the rest."

Christopher nodded.

"I've come up with something else I'd like to do in addition to lowering my interest rates."

He paused and smiled a little timidly, an altogether new and childlike expression on the face of the former Mammon-loving banker.

"I hope you don't think it's silly of me, Mr. Braxton," he said, with something like a nervous chuckle, "to try to base so much on one particular story I read in the Bible."

"Believe me, I find it far from silly," replied Christopher. "I find your experience to represent the very essence of the walk of faith."

"Never has anything I've read spoken so personally and directly to me," said the banker enthusiastically. "I do not think I exaggerate when I say that the story of that rich man Zacchaeus quite literally has changed my whole outlook on what it means to be a Christian. Suddenly it's all so . . . so very practical, so here and now. It is exactly as you said in that sermon of yours—it's so *do-able*."

"I'm glad you find it so, Franklin. I have always found the Christian life the most down-to-earth of all possible creeds, and the four Gospels the most practical of all guidebooks."

"In any event," the banker went on, "I would like to begin giving twenty percent of all my bank's income to the church."

"Twenty percent!"

"Lowering my rates was the first thing I felt I ought to do. Now perhaps this will be the secondfold action on my part, so to speak."

"How do you mean *secondfold*?"

"Just as Zacchaeus did. I intend to continue praying that God would show me what threefold and fourfold ways I might return some of my money to this community."

Christopher took in the words with a solemn sense of awe at the fact that this man before him was now seeking God's guidance for every decision of his life.

"Franklin," Christopher said, "I would like to ask you a question. Do you in any way feel that this giving will make things different between you and God?"

"Ah, I see what you mean," replied Mr. Royce. "No, I know that God accepts me as I am and for who I am. These are things I *want* to do."

"But if I may ask another question," said Christopher after a brief pause, "you don't, do you, feel as though you have taken from anyone *falsely* or *wrongly*, as in the story of Zacchaeus?"

"Perhaps not in so many words," replied Mr. Royce. "I do not know that I ever broke the law, if that is what you mean. But my motive was entirely for myself and not for my neighbor. My intent was to squeeze as much profit from this community as I possibly could. So whereas perhaps I did not intentionally swindle my customers, I nevertheless profited more than was proper. I grew rich while the people of this community labored to eke out their sometimes less-than-modest livings. It was not right. So what other con-clusion is to be drawn but that I did wrong?"

"Yet perhaps the fourfold repayment of Zacchaeus is more than is required in your case."

"Perhaps. But all my life I have been giving *less* than is required. Why should I not now give *more* than is required. Does ever a man suffer from giving too much to God?"

Christopher smiled. "No, Franklin," he said. "No, I suppose not."

"And besides, I'm enjoying my money now far more than I ever did letting it gather dust and interest in all my various invest-ments!"

"Well then—I heartily endorse your plan. In fact, I think it would greatly encourage the town for you to share the impact this Scripture has had upon you one Sunday evening."

"Oh no," rejoined Mr. Royce quickly. "No one must know of this. It must remain just between us two."

"Of course, I will respect your wishes if that is your desire. But may I ask why?"

Again a sheepish expression came over the banker's face.

"I'm afraid you will eventually think me silly," he said, "if in everything I point to some Scripture or other. But I must confess that two or three days ago I was reading—again in the Gospels, just as you recommended, although this time in Matthew—when Jesus spoke about how we are to give. You are no doubt familiar with the passage."

Christopher nodded knowingly, sensing what was coming.

"He said something like, 'Make sure when you give to the poor, that you don't do it to be seen by other men. Don't blow a trumpet when you do good like the Pharisees and hypocrites do. Don't even let your left hand know what your right hand is doing. Do it in secret so only God will see it.' Those are my own words, of course, but that is something like it."

"I am familiar with the passage," smiled Christopher. "You have captured its meaning, I think, very accurately."

"If ever there was a Pharisee and a hypocrite," Mr. Royce went on, "it was me—though I cannot say I ever did much giving in my life, even *to* be seen by others. So if I am going to make a new start,

I certainly don't intend to blow a trumpet and announce it, as it says."

"Then I will happily respect your wishes," replied Christopher. "But tell me—why do you then come to tell me of it now?"

"Because if I merely deposited money into the church's family-tithe account, one day it would certainly come to your notice that there was far more money present than you had deposited. I'm sure you believe in the principle of the loaves and the fishes, but you are also a practical man, Mr. Braxton, and I have no doubt you would investigate the thing, possibly mentioning it to the church committee before coming to me, and the whole affair would come out."

"I see," laughed Christopher. "You have thought of everything!"

"Now that I have you in on my little scheme, so to speak, I will be free to add to the account, and you will be free to make use of the account, without anyone else sharing our secret."

"I must say, Franklin," laughed Christopher, "you are proving as shrewd in your obedience to the Scriptures as you have been as a businessman."

"Isn't there something about being wise as serpents but innocent as doves?"

"Indeed there is!"

"And I would ask one more thing of you, Mr. Braxton . . . er, Christopher," said the banker.

"Name it."

"That if a need should arise in the community, or on the part of any individual, which cannot be met by the church fund, or which you feel would not be an appropriate expenditure, I would ask that you come to me in confidence and share it with me. There may be some way in which I can help."

"The third and fourthfold repayment you spoke of?"

Mr. Royce nodded. "Though such was always my goal up until a very short time ago, I do not want to die a rich man. Therefore I must find worthy means to dispose of my wealth gradually and quietly and without show. I can think of no more worthy means than investing in the lives of those in need."

"I will certainly do as you ask, Franklin," replied Christopher, fighting back the tears that now sought to rise in his eyes.

Mr. Royce stood and the two men shook hands, almost as if they were now business colleagues who had entered into a new agreement. In truth, as Christopher said when he told me of the interview, it was an eternal partnership in the affairs of the kingdom.

CHAPTER 44

LEARNING TO WAIT

It was on a Sunday midway through the fall of that year when Christopher shared another very personal message from his heart. This one had more to do with me.

"Ever since Corrie and my decision to remain here in Miracle Springs," he began, "I have been struggling within my own heart to understand the events leading up to that decision. I have said nothing publicly about it, and actually, Corrie and I have not spoken about it a great deal either.

"To be perfectly honest, I have been embarrassed about this and have felt the need to understand it myself before being able to talk to anyone else about it. At last I have come to feel some perspective dawning which I would like to share this morning with you—and with my dear wife too," he added, looking at me with a smile. "I have stressed the necessity of obedience so frequently that I hope this will be helpful to you in those circumstances in which you are uncertain about what exactly obedience might mean."

He paused to collect his thoughts, took in a couple of breaths, then continued.

"Oftentimes for the Christian man or woman, the Lord's leading in a certain direction is very quiet and subtle at first," he said. "You begin simply to *sense* something stirring deep in the hidden regions of your mind or heart. Have any of you had that experience?"

He paused, and a few heads nodded.

"You might not even know what it is at first," Christopher went

209

on. "It *may* be the beginning of the Lord's leading, or it may *not* be. But it has been my experience that if it *is* the Lord's voice, that sense will gradually grow stronger over the next weeks and months. If it is not, then gradually it will go away.

"Now when that sense I speak of does begin to grow stronger, two more things begin to happen. They move you closer to the point of one day being able to say you are confident that you *are* hearing God's voice and that you are thus ready to *do* what he is telling you.

"The first of these factors is—*specificity.* The gradual sense you felt initially in an undefined way becomes more and more specific. Instead of just having a vague feeling, you find your thoughts beginning to focus on something specific to *do.*

"The second factor has to do with *circumstances.* Events and situations begin to line up in your life in such a way as to make the doing of that specific thing possible.

"All right, are you with me so far?" he asked, glancing around the church. "First comes a feeling of some direction, followed by specificity and circumstances which ultimately will make obedience possible." He continued to wait a moment more.

"Now let me tell you how this worked for me last year," he went on. "At first I began to feel a vague sense that perhaps my days of ministry were not over after all, as I had previously thought. As I continued to pray, this sense grew stronger. I eventually began to feel what I thought was the Lord saying that a time was coming when I would serve him in a new place in a new way. You see, the sense that I first felt grew gradually stronger and more specific."

Christopher stopped and smiled.

"It was all going according to the proper order up to this point. But then . . . I made a mistake," he said. "I put the cart before the horse, so to speak. *Circumstances* hadn't yet developed in my life to focus that leading into some *specific* direction and toward some *definite* course of action the Lord wanted me to follow.

"So what did I do? I'm embarrassed to say it, but I now realize that I went out on my own, *without* the Lord's leading, and tried to manufacture my *own* set of circumstances into which I then tried to fit the partial leading that had come to me at the time.

"Time, patience, and *waiting* upon the Lord—these are all critical elements in discerning and obeying the Lord's voice. Sometimes the specificity and the circumstances take a long while to develop. If we're not careful, having received a preliminary sense in a given direction, we can go charging off prematurely on our own without waiting for the rest of God's leading. In so doing we leave the Lord and his guidance behind.

"This is exactly what I did. What I thought I heard from the Lord was indeed accurate—he *was* preparing to use me in a new place in a new way. I think I was hearing his voice in a true direction. But I did not wait. I began to infuse into that leading my *own* interpretation of what I concluded God must be planning to do.

"I did not wait for circumstances to confirm God's direction, I acted impatiently and created my own circumstances. And as you all know—Corrie best of all—I began making plans for us to return to the East, because that was how I assumed he intended to carry out the leading I had felt.

"Of course, we all realize now that I was wrong. Circumstances did eventually come, in this case sad circumstances for us all, which prevented my continuing on my mistake and brought me back to the specific course of action the Lord intended all along— which was to remain right here among you in Miracle Springs."

Christopher paused again and glanced at me with an earnest and loving expression.

"I would therefore," he went on, "like to take this opportunity to apologize to all of you, and especially to you, Corrie, for my impatience at the time, and for putting you through that period of uncertainty. I was wrong. I had stepped out from under the Lord's guiding hand, and I am truly and humbly sorry."

I smiled back at Christopher and nodded slightly. If I had any need to forgive him, I had done so long before.

CHAPTER 45

TWO KINDS OF OBEDIENCE

"You see, friends," Christopher now went on, "it is possible to hear the Lord *correctly*, but in our impatience to obey *wrongly*. Several months ago I spoke to you about the need to obey promptly when the way before you is clear. If you have wronged someone, for example, to delay restitution is to disobey. Obedience in such a case must be swift and immediate.

"But in other situations, such as this which I faced where the specificity of the obedience was *not* yet clear, waiting is a vital and necessary component of the obedience. I was doing my best to walk in the light I had at the time. But I did not yet have the full light of God's direction, so to act was premature.

"The revelation was a growing one, and I needed to give it time to develop within me until the path the Lord was laying out was clear. This is not to say that there are not times when you must step out in obedience in the face of uncertainties. Yet often we must wait patiently for more light.

"Earlier this year I did the one when I should have been doing the other. I did a thing that is sometimes a right and proper thing to do. I believe my motives were honest. But in my impatience, I stepped out too hastily ahead of the leading. I got God's message mixed up.

"Now, did I *sin* in what I did?

"Perhaps not, I don't know. I did not so much do *wrong* as make an honest mistake. I mistook the specifics of God's initial leading. I should have listened more attentively to the reservations Corrie was voicing at the time. You see, that was a circumstance too—the fact that Corrie felt uncomfortable about the proposed move. But by then I had already convinced myself that we were to go another direction. My failure to listen to her caused tension between us ... yet another circumstance I should have heeded, for when the Lord is truly leading, tension ought not to be present.

"As I now look back, I can see all sorts of warning signals indicating that I was mistaken. Yet somehow I was blind to them at the time."

Christopher stopped and took a deep breath.

"Now, there are two important questions this brings up," he went on. "One, how do you tell the difference between these two kinds of leading from God—when you should obey instantly and when you must wait for further clarification of specifics and circumstances? And two, what do you do if and when you realize you *have* made a mistake?

"Let me address the second question first.

"When you've made a mistake, the most important thing is to summon the courage to go back and undo it. As difficult as it might be, apologize where you need to, then start out fresh by trying to hear God's voice accurately. You may have to undo a decision you've already made, as we did. Our tickets were already bought and paid for!" he laughed.

"It may mean that you will have to be willing to look foolish. Imagine the embarrassment, for example, of being at the wedding altar and suddenly realizing the whole thing is a mistake! Yet better to admit it, egg on your face and all, than to base a marriage on something other than God's leading.

"I can tell you I have felt something like that many times this year. Here I am your pastor, and yet my very being here in this pulpit began with a huge blunder on my part. I cannot recall it now without a certain lingering sense of humiliation.

"But that is part of our human weakness. We *do* make mistakes. I will make many more as your pastor, and I hope you will continue to be forgiving and patient with me. I am struggling to understand how to live my Christian faith just as are all of you. Yet looking foolish is still better than going ahead with a mistaken decision.

"For imagine what the consequences might have been had I

214

been too stubborn and proud to admit my mistake. Corrie and I would now be in the East, lonely and probably miserable. I would probably not be pastoring, or if I had managed to find a church my ministry would be ineffective because I would not be where the Lord had planned for me to be. My ministry would be based not upon the Lord's leading, but upon my impatience. And you here in Miracle Springs would not have the pastor God intended for you.

"This is not to say that God cannot redeem situations and turn them to good in spite of our mistakes. He certainly can and does. But my point is that we can perpetuate a great deal of mischief and heartache in our own lives and in the lives of others when we are not willing to retrace our steps and humbly listen for *his* voice instead of our own."

Christopher paused. "Imagine yourself walking through a stretch of forest in the hills east of here, trying to get back home," he said. "If the path you are on is an unfamiliar one, and suddenly you realize you have taken a wrong turn, what is the quickest way back here to Miracle Springs? Clearly it is to turn around and go back to wherever you made a wrong turn. To keep going on the wrong path will only take you further and further from where you are trying to get.

"Do you see what I mean? Sometimes to keep moving forward is the worst thing to do. Progress in such a case lies only in turning around to get back on the right path that leads back down out of the mountains to where you are trying to get. Such is, I believe, the importance of being able to admit our mistakes."

Christopher paused, took out his watch, and glanced down at it.

"Ten to twelve," he said, smiling. "Give me another five minutes, and we will be done."

"Take as long as you want, son!" Pa called out from the front row.

"I appreciate your support, Drum," rejoined Christopher. "But everyone may not agree with you."

"Then they can lodge their complaints with me!"

"I think five minutes will do it," laughed Christopher. "All right," he went on, "now to the other question I asked—how do you know the difference between situations where you must obey quickly and those where you must wait?"

He paused for his question to sink in.

"Actually," he said after a moment, "I think it is rather a simple distinction. I doubt it will even take the full five minutes! Where doing good toward some other individual is involved, then I say obey without delay. Has the Lord put before you the opportunity to show some kindness, to speak a gracious word, to forgive, to serve? Then do it now.

"There is no use waiting and pondering in prayer, *O Lord, wouldst thou have me exercise kindness and do a good deed toward this soul you have placed before me, or wouldst thou have me wait and keep my kindnesses to myself, and pray for thy guidance?*"

I could hear some laughing as Christopher said it!

"Such is a Pharisee's prayer," he went on. "Is there a kindness to do? Do it! Is there forgiveness to be asked? Ask it! Is the way from Scripture clear? Then obey the Lord's words immediately and daily.

"But, on the other hand, do you face a decision that involves not a clear good toward your neighbor, but rather a direction in your own life? Then I say this may be occasion for waiting. *Either* direction may bring good, yet you do not know which of two courses the Lord would have you pursue. Then it is time to wait patiently for specific circumstances to unfold.

"It may be a choice between two equally good options. Then wait for the Lord, continue to pray, and do not force events, as I did, with circumstances of your own devising.

"You see, friends, the Christian walk of faith, while the simplest of lives, is also one of the most complex. If we were given a mere set of rules, as is the case with many of the world's religions, such uncertainties as we have been speaking about this morning would not exist. But our Father has made us his sons and daughters, not his slaves, and as such he instructs us to walk by faith, not by sight. Therein sometimes lies the difficulty of being a Christian, but at the same time, the wonderful and glorious challenge. Shall we pray together?

"*Our dear Father,*" Christopher prayed, "*we are so thankful for the life of faith you have given us as your sons and daughters. We thank you that you lead and guide and speak to us. And we thank you that you allow us a part in listening and interpreting and learning to perceive your voice. As weak as we are, you yet trust us to hear you and obey you. Increase our capacity, Lord, to hear you rightly and to obey your voice truly. Help us to obey with hasty and unhesitant love toward our neighbors, and help us to obey with patient waiting when you speak new directions into our personal lives. We thank you, Father, that your ways toward us are always good, always loving, and that in all things we may trust you. Amen."*

CHAPTER 46

GOOD TEARS AND GOODBYES

I suppose down inside I knew that we couldn't keep living in the bunkhouse forever. That's fine when a husband and wife are just starting out. But eventually you want a place of your own where you can raise a family, a place that you can call your very own home. As much as I loved being so close to my family, I knew that time would come for Christopher and me too.

Pa and Christopher had talked about building a new house on Pa's property with Christopher's share of the money from the mine, and even about us buying enough land from Pa that we could have plenty of room to call our own. And no doubt Mr. Royce would have happily lent us money now if we wanted to build a new house. I hoped we would do that someday because I wanted to live near Pa and Almeda just like Uncle Nick and Aunt Katie did. It felt good and safe to have a community of people close by who could love and watch out for one another.

But for right now, building a new house didn't seem to be what we were supposed to do. With Christopher pastoring the church now, we felt it was important that he be as accessible to the congregation as possible. It had already come up a time or two in conversation about the benefit to the church if we could live in town.

As we did speak of it more, it was always in connection with the church and our role among the people as the pastor and his wife. Gradually I think both Christopher and I came to realize that we were not the ones who were supposed to buy the freight company from Pa and Almeda. I wasn't sure Becky and Tad were going to want it either. I knew that in her heart Becky still wanted to marry someday. And Tad still talked with wide eyes about going to sea. So the future of the business remained in doubt.

It was around the first of October that Mr. Duncan's purchase of the Perkins farm was made final. Mr. Duncan and his family had been renting Almeda's house in town, the one where she lived before she married Pa. Now, within a month, that house would be vacant. That's when Christopher and I began talking seriously and praying about whether it was time for us to set up housekeeping on our own.

Even though I could tell part of her didn't want us to leave any more than part of me wanted to, it was Almeda who brought it up the moment she knew the Duncans would be moving out. She said that if we wanted it, the house was available to us.

We both knew immediately that it was the right thing to do. We wouldn't have to go through all the work of building a new place at the same time Christopher was doing all he could to establish his new ministry on the right foot. Since the church had made him pastor, he'd been spending lots of his free time visiting and calling on people, getting to know everyone in the community and finding out what their needs were and how he could help them. He didn't want to interrupt that process anytime soon with thoughts of building a new house. And being in town would not only make the calling easier, but would make him more accessible for work as well. It was important, too, he said, that he continue to put in his fair share of time working at the mine when he didn't have other work.

All things considered, we decided to make the move as soon as the Duncans were settled in their new place.

At last the day came in the second week of November, just the week after Mr. Grant's election as the new President of the United States.

Christopher and I loaded up the things of ours that were in the bunkhouse—our bed, a chest of drawers, a small oak writing table, our clothes—as well as a bureau, a secretary, and a few other things from the big house that Pa and Almeda wanted to give us. Then there were boxes and crates of house things, linens and utensils and cooking pots.

Midway through the morning, Harriet Rutledge rode up in her buggy. Christopher and I were outside and had just put a couple of chairs up on the wagon. Harriet got down, then grabbed a small box and carried it over toward us, setting it on the back of the wagon.

"What's this?" Christopher asked.

"My contribution to your move," she replied.

Christopher and I glanced at each other with puzzled expressions. Christopher lifted the cover that lay over the top of the box and peered inside.

"Books?" he said.

"Yes," replied Harriet. "I've been waiting for the right opportunity to tell you, and now that you two are going to have your own place, I want you to have Avery's books."

"But . . ." began Christopher, too astonished to know what to say.

"It is just what he would want," Harriet went on. "I want you to have my husband's library. I just brought this box as a token. When you are moved in, we will transfer all the rest."

Christopher was silent. I knew tears were trying to rise in his eyes.

"Harriet," he said finally, "I just don't know what to say. It's too generous and wonderful a thing for me to be able to respond to."

"Books are nothing if they are not used," she answered. "Books are not to gather dust; they are to be taken down and thumbed through and read and learned and grown from. You will give Avery's library its best and hardest use. You know how happy that would make him. Most of the books on theology came from Mr. Henderson, as you know. They came into our hands when he died, now they can pass into *your* hands. Possessions are never permanent. God gives them to us for a season. Therefore, *use* them, Christopher, with my blessing. It will make me happy too."

Christopher smiled, then nodded.

"Thank you, Harriet. It will be an honor. I will call it my Avery Rutledge Library, and I will think of him every time I open one of them—which, I promise you, will be almost a daily occurrence."

Everyone helped us load our belongings into Pa's flatbed wagon. There was a fun and playful spirit as we tramped back and forth from the house and bunkhouse to the wagon, carrying and lifting, people asking if we were taking this or that . . . laughing and joking and gaiety.

Yet underneath the happiness there was a sadness too. I suppose I knew it was there, but I didn't want to think about it for fear I would start crying.

Of course I was excited to think of moving into a new home that would be just for Christopher and me. But I would miss all this too. From now on, whenever I came here, I would be a visitor. There was another place I would call home. It might not always even be Almeda's house in town. But wherever it was, "home" would never be here again.

I was thirty-one years old, happily married, and at last leaving the roof of my father for a roof my husband and I would call *ours*.

The time had come when Christopher and I would make *home* something we shared only between us, and with what family the Lord chose to honor us with.

It could not help, therefore, be a melancholy moment. I loved this place. It was the only home I had known for more than half my life.

I knew Almeda was thinking similar thoughts.

I turned from hoisting a box of kitchen things up onto the wagon and began walking back to the house. There was Almeda standing near the porch. She had been watching me and now stood still, holding one corner of her apron to her face. Becky and I had already hugged and cried two or three times, and somehow the parting didn't seem so momentous with her. But Almeda and I had not spoken our goodbyes yet.

I now walked toward her. There were tears in her eyes.

I approached and without a word went straight into her arms. We remained there, both weeping softly. They were tears of sadness, yet good tears too. It was a necessary thing that was happening, a part of life's process of growth.

We stood apart. Almeda's hands were on my shoulders. She looked me full in the face, smiling through her red eyes and tears.

"Corrie . . . Corrie!" she sighed softly. "Just look at you now. You're a grown woman, married, and embarking on a life of your own."

"Did you ever think it would happen?" I said, half laughing through my own tears.

"What?"

"That I would be married and have a home of my own."

"Of course."

"I sure never did."

Almeda smiled.

"I knew it would happen all along," she said. "The whole world of men would have been fools to pass up as fine a young lady as you, Corrie Belle Hollister Braxton!"

I returned her smile. "Be honest," I said. "Did you *really* know?"

Almeda nodded. "I knew the Lord was saving you for just the right man."

We stood another few seconds, holding each other's eyes.

"I'm going to miss you, Corrie," said Almeda softly, her eyes filling with tears again.

"And I'll miss you," I said. "You're the best friend I ever had . . . until Christopher came along. I'll never forget all you've done for me."

"You have been a treasure to me, Corrie . . . a gift from God. You have helped make my life so rich."

"Oh, Almeda . . ." I said, starting to cry again. How do you find the words to tell someone like that how much you love her? "It isn't as if I'm going far away," I said. "We'll still see each other . . . every day."

"Right," laughed Almeda, trying hard to smile, just like I was. "Of course . . . nothing has to change."

Inside, however, I think we both knew that after this day things could not help but change. We would love each other just as much, and we would always remain just as close . . . but it would be different. You can never go back and recapture what some things were like when you were young.

That's one of the things about growing up—there's a melancholy that comes with it when you look back at how things used to be.

"Corrie!" a shout sounded behind me.

I turned. There was Christopher running toward us.

I turned back toward Almeda, then embraced her one last time. "I love you, Almeda," I whispered.

"Oh, Corrie . . . I love you so much," I heard her reply softly in my ear. Then her arms pulled me tight and I could feel her strong embrace all around me. "May God give you the best life imaginable!"

"Thank you," I whispered. I squeezed her once more, then we released one another, and I turned toward the new best friend God had given me—the husband who had given me his name, and to whom I had given my life and my love.

CHAPTER 47

NEW START IN OUR OWN HOME

When the wagon was all loaded and the team hitched up, Christopher helped me up to the seat, then jumped up after me.

"We'll follow you into town to help with the unloading," said Pa.

"Give us an hour or so," said Christopher. "We'd like to be alone for just a while there together."

"All right, but just don't do any of the heavy lifting till me and Tad get there."

"I promise."

"Are you two going to sleep in town tonight?" asked Almeda, "or will you be back out?"

"We'll have to see how moved in we are," I answered.

"You'll have supper here with us?"

"That we will agree to!" said Christopher.

"I'll make up one of the extra beds, just in case," said Almeda.

Christopher flicked the reins, and the wagon jostled into motion behind the two horses.

" 'Bye!" came choruses of voices behind us.

We all waved, Christopher and I in the wagon, and the rest of the family standing by the house in a group watching us go. They were still standing there, hands in the air, as we rounded the hilltop and went out of sight.

I turned back around toward the front, slipped my arm through Christopher's, snuggled close to him. We rode most of the rest of the way into Miracle Springs in silence. There were a lot of things to think about. It was a time of change for us, and we both were aware of it.

Twenty-five or thirty minutes later we pulled up in front of the house that to most folks in town was still known as "the Parrish place," in honor of Almeda's first husband who had built it after they had arrived in California from Boston.

Christopher set the brake on the wheel, then jumped to the ground and helped me down beside him. He ran to the door, opened it, and ran back to where I was standing.

Without so much as a warning, he suddenly reached around my waist with one hand and under my knees with the other and scooped me off my feet.

"What are you doing?" I exclaimed.

"Merely complying with tradition, my dear," he replied.

Holding me in his arms as though I weighed no more than a feather, Christopher walked toward the house, then sideways through the door.

"I know we're not newlyweds anymore," he said, "but since this is our first real home together, I thought it only fitting that I carry you across the threshold."

"Oh, Christopher . . . you are a romantic!"

"And I hope I will always remain one—that is, if you don't tire of me."

"Never!"

He walked into the big, empty sitting room, stopped, and slowly turned me all the way around as we gazed upon the place where we would start the years of our life together. For several long moments we remained there, silent with our own thoughts.

"Well, Mrs. Braxton," Christopher said at length, still holding me in his arms. "I think we're home."

He bent his face down and kissed me gently. As he eased back from me I threw my arms around his neck and hugged him tight.

"I am so glad you picked me up off that road by Mrs. Timms' farm," I whispered into his ear. "I can't imagine now that I lived so many years of my life without knowing you."

Christopher laughed.

"I know what you mean. It seems like we've known each other forever, doesn't it?"

I sighed contentedly.

"Oh, Christopher," I murmured. "I am so happy to be your wife, and to be able to share the rest of life with you."

"I share your happiness," he said. "But I'm getting the best of the bargain."

"How so?" I asked.

"Just look at all the Lord has blessed me with—the finest woman a man could ever want for a wife—"

"Oh, go on!"

"I mean it—you are! But let me finish."

"I promise not to interrupt again."

"All right then. He's given me a wife, a home to call my own, even though it's not *really* mine—"

"It may be someday."

"Perhaps."

"Almeda said we could buy it from her anytime we wanted, for no more than it cost Mr. Parrish to build it eighteen years ago."

"She's a generous woman—we'll see. But you said you wouldn't interrupt again!"

"You asked about the house!" I laughed.

"I did no such thing. In any case, God has given me a wife, a house, a partial stake in a gold mine, a family with brothers and sisters and aunts and uncles and a father-in-law and whatever Almeda is to me who all love and accept me . . . and in addition a church to pastor.

"Goodness, Corrie! In all my wildest dreams, I never expected to be so blessed if I lived to be a hundred. When I met Corrie Belle Hollister, it was like discovering three or four pots of gold at the end of the rainbow . . . all at once!"

By now I was laughing again. I couldn't help it.

"So do you see why I say I got the best of the bargain? I got all that, and all you received in exchange was a man—a penniless husband of soiled pastoral reputation."

Again I wrapped my arms around Christopher's neck, kissed him on the cheek, and then murmured into his ear.

"But what a man I got!" I said. "A man of God! And that is

worth more to a woman than any ten gold mines or twenty houses!"

A moment more we remained in silence, then Christopher gently eased me down to the floor.

We stood for a minute in the middle of the room, arm in arm, without saying anything more.

"We are going to have a good life here, Christopher," I said at length. "God is going to bless this home."

When Christopher finally opened his mouth, he was not speaking to me.

"*Father,*" he prayed, "*we want to take this opportunity again, as we have done in the past, to dedicate our lives, our future, our marriage, our ministry together, and this home and all that takes place under this roof . . . to you. We join our hearts and pray that you would accomplish good here through us. May hearts and lives be changed as the men and women of this community come to know you more intimately.*"

He paused a moment, then continued.

"*Most of all, Father,*" he prayed, "*accomplish your purposes in our hearts and lives. Transform us. Make us fully your son and your daughter, for we desire nothing but that the life of your Spirit flow in us and through us. Let us serve the people of this community. Give us opportunities not to be highly thought of, but to minister the foot-washing example of Christlike servanthood to the people who come our way. May this home be a refuge for all who enter its doors, where they may find peace, acceptance, truth, and love . . . and most of all where they may find your loving Fatherhood toward them. Give us obedient and humble hearts to do your will. Deepen within us the desire to seek after nothing but your will. We look to you, our Father, to supply our every need, and to make known the course you want our footsteps to take. We give ourselves completely to you, Father.*"

He stopped, and it was silent again.

"*Amen,*" I said.

Yet a few seconds longer we stood.

"Well, what do you say, Mrs. Braxton?" said Christopher, turning toward me. "Shall we unload that wagon and begin turning this place into the home of Corrie and Christopher Braxton?"

ABOUT THE AUTHOR

MICHAEL PHILLIPS is one of the premier fiction authors publishing in the Christian marketplace. He has authored more than fifty books, with total sales exceeding 4 million copies. He is also well known as the editor of the popular George MacDonald Classics series.

Phillips owns and operates a Christian bookstore on the West Coast. He and his wife, Judy, live with their three grown sons in Eureka, California.

If you liked *A New Beginning* and *The Braxtons of Miracle Springs,* you may also enjoy these other books and series by Michael Phillips:

THE JOURNALS OF CORRIE BELLE HOLLISTER
(Bethany House Publishers)

> *My Father's World* (with Judith Pella)
> *Daughter of Grace* (with Judith Pella)
> *On the Trail of the Truth*
> *A Place in the Sun*
> *Sea to Shining Sea*
> *Into the Long Dark Night*
> *Land of the Brave and the Free*
> *A Home for the Heart*
> *Grayfox*

TALES FROM SCOTLAND AND RUSSIA
(Bethany House Publishers)

Adventuresome, dramatic, and mysterious stories from the romantic worlds of nineteenth-century Scotland and Russia. Coauthored with Judith Pella, these books are packed with abiding spiritual truths and memorable relationships. If you haven't yet discovered the worlds of adventure and intrigue opened up by these series, a wonderful treat awaits you!

Scotland:
> *Heather Hills of Stonewycke*
> *Flight From Stonewycke*
> *The Lady of Stonewycke*

Stranger at Stonewycke
Shadows Over Stonewycke
Treasure of Stonewycke

Jamie MacLeod, Highland Lass
Robbie Taggart, Highland Sailor

Russia:
The Crown and the Crucible
A House Divided
Travail and Triumph

THE SECRET OF THE ROSE (Tyndale House Publishers)

The Eleventh Hour
A Rose Remembered
Escape to Freedom
Dawn of Liberty

MERCY AND EAGLEFLIGHT (Tyndale House Publishers)

This is the newest series from the pen of Michael Phillips, set in 1890s Kansas

Mercy and Eagle Flight
A Dangerous Love
Goodness and Mercy

NONFICTION BY MICHAEL PHILLIPS
A God to Call Father
Good Things to Remember
Best Friends for Life (with Judy Phillips)

THE WORKS OF GEORGE MACDONALD
(Bethany House Publishers)

Twenty-eight books edited by Michael Phillips, both fiction *and* nonfiction, that will delight and edify both adult and young readers. Please consult your bookstore or write for a full list of availability. Especially recommended titles include:

Fiction by George MacDonald Edited for Today's Reader:
The Fisherman's Lady
The Baronet's Song
The Curate's Awakening
The Highlander's Last Song
The Laird's Inheritance

Nonfiction From the Writings of George MacDonald:
Discovering the Character of God
Knowing the Heart of God
George MacDonald, Scotland's Beloved Storyteller
    (a biography of MacDonald by Michael Phillips)

Finding a Godly Spouse

Bold and Practical Help for Young People and Their Parents.

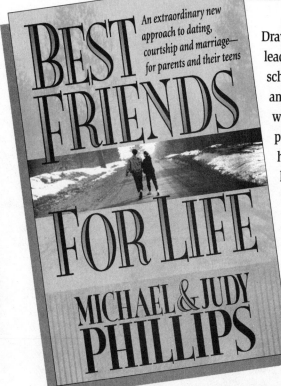

An extraordinary new approach to dating, courtship and marriage—for parents and their teens

BEST FRIENDS FOR LIFE

MICHAEL & JUDY PHILLIPS

Drawing upon their years of leadership in the home-school movement, Michael and Judy Phillips offer wise, balanced, and practical counsel about how to find godly husbands and wives in their new book, *Best Friends for Life.*

From the author of the CORRIE BELLE HOLLISTER series